LUCKY'S NAUGHTY ANGEL

A SECOND CHANCE ROMANCE - DREAMS FULFILLED BOOK TWO

SCARLETT KING

HOT AND STEAMY ROMANCE

CONTENTS

Sign Up to Receive Free Books	v
Blurb	vii
1. Chapter One	1
2. Chapter Two	9
3. Chapter Three	16
4. Chapter Four	23
5. Chapter Five	37
6. Chapter Six	44
7. Chapter Seven	56
8. Chapter Eight	64
9. Chapter Nine	70
10. Chapter Ten	75
Sign Up to Receive Free Books	83
Preview of A Kiss of Winter	85
Chapter 1	88
Chapter 2	95
Chapter 3	104
Other Books By This Author	115
Copyright	117

Made in "The United States by:

Scarlett King

© Copyright 2020 – Scarlett King

ISBN: 978-1-64808-027-2

ALL RIGHTS RESERVED. No part of this publication may be reproduced or transmitted in any form whatsoever, electronic, or mechanical, including photocopying, recording, or by any informational storage or retrieval system without express written, dated and signed permission from the author

❦ Created with Vellum

SIGN UP TO RECEIVE FREE BOOKS

Sign Up to Receive Free E-Books and Audiobook Codes.

Would you like to read **The Unexpected Nanny, Dirty Little Virgin** and **other romance books** for **free**?

You can sign up to receive these free e-books and audiobooks by typing this link into your browser:

https://www.steamyromance.info/free-books-and-audiobooks-hot-and-steamy/

Or this one:

https://www.steamyromance.info/the-unexpected-nanny-free/

BLURB

Aaron "Lucky" Gates never really had much luck—in love or in life. Dragged into a biker gang by a combination of desperation and pressure from his reckless older brother, Daniel, Aaron took the fall for an assault Daniel committed and spent ten years behind bars. Now, he's a bouncer at Phoenicia's only nightspot, struggling to rebuild his life while his brother keeps trying to coax him back into the gang. The one bright spot in his life, besides his friends at the job and his rescue dog Moose, is the sweet, beautiful girl he volunteers alongside at the church.

Two problems: she's only twenty-one, and she's Reverend Alderson's daughter. He's headed toward forty and has no business sniffing around a girl who's so pure she could probably draw a whole herd of unicorns. Or so he thinks.

Julia sees things a bit differently. She looks at Aaron and sees a great big lonely bear of a man who not only attracts her, but makes her feel safe. She wants her father to understand, but knows it may be years before he does. And though she's a good person, she's not as innocent as the men in her life want to believe.

CHAPTER ONE

Aaron

Every day that I wake up a free man, I take a deep breath and thank God for it. Sometimes it takes me a minute to remember where I am, but it all comes back to me when I open my eyes and see my neat little trailer around me instead of a cage. But before I can even do that, I'm stuck shaking off the shadows of the past.

The guys at the bar would be shocked to learn that their six-foot-six bouncer, who once flipped a patron's MINI Cooper onto its roof when he wouldn't pay his tab, regularly wakes up gasping—shaking like a kid waking up from a nightmare. But that's me, every damn morning.

The worst part is that hazy instant before the nightmare lets go of me. For just that moment, I expect that I'll open my eyes and see the cell around me instead of my home, and I'll know that being free was just a dream, and I'm still in that same damned cage that I lived in for ten years.

My personal Hell is a real place on earth—that tiny prison cell where the lights would always glare down, shared with three other orange jumpsuits. In that Hell, even though I knew I could flatten any of them, two of the three would leave me with scars.

Every morning the remembered nightmare recedes into the darkest parts of my head—where it belongs. This morning I sit up slowly, rubbing my eyes as the comforter slithers down my bare chest. It takes a few moments for my heart to stop pounding.

It's cold in my trailer. I usually turn the heat off in the early hours and rely on my thick down comforters instead. That way I don't have to dig into my savings by the end of the month just to pay for propane. Fortunately, even without a woman in my life, I've got some help keeping the bed warm.

Moose looks up from the foot of the king-sized mattress barely squeezed into the trailer's sleeping alcove. The big dog yawns and whines, thumping his tail. I reach over and scuff his floppy, chocolate-colored ears. He's a bit like me: a giant, muscular mutt that finally got out of his cage.

First thing I did once I finished parole was rescue Moose from the pound, so I would always have company that understands me. He and I took a road trip Upstate to live in the trailer on land that used to belong to my buddy Jake. It's tough to start over with a felony on your record, so I went back to the one place where people actually know I'm not a bad guy: the town I grew up in.

Phoenicia's a bitty touristy town in the middle of nowhere in the Catskills, so different from the halfway house in the Bronx and the Hell I left behind that I don't really fit in here anymore. I'm a giant tattooed biker with a touch of a Bronx accent now; you would never know that I grew up here.

Fortunately, the owner of the local bar is an old friend from school, just like Jake. He even rides himself on weekends, and he was looking for a big, intimidating guy to be his bouncer. That job, along with the place to stay, saved my life as much as the dog and my friends.

Phoenicia is pretty—clean streets, a selection of restaurants, even a couple of spots that are open after ten, which is rare around here. I make some of the tourists nervous when I wander around, especially with the big dog, so I do my best to soften my image. Sit down, talk quiet, smile. Leave the armor I grew in prison—which I started forming on the road even earlier—aside.

It only works sometimes, so I spend more of my time alone than I would prefer. Especially when it comes to women. The ladies who go to Eddy's bar know that, drunk or sober, they're safer with me around than without. Now and again, I get to take one home. But it's always a casual thing for them. Phoenicia considers itself high-end, so almost nobody wants a working-class boyfriend with a record.

Moose hops down and shakes himself, knocking me out of my reverie, and I scoot out of bed and stand up, stretching carefully. I tend to knock my knuckles on the trailer ceiling if I don't watch it.

I've spent years taking practical steps toward rebuilding my life: fixing up the trailer, then buying it, then buying the land. Only then, did I move on from my original Harley and dog trailer to a big red cruiser with a sidecar, so Moose can ride in style. He even has his own helmet and goggles. The local kids love watching us roll through town.

I spend a good part of my days working now, too—sort of. Volunteering at the church every week is as much for me as anyone else. It's hard to keep thinking of yourself as a complete piece of shit once you wear yourself out delivering meals, fixing a poor local's window, or digging their car out.

I sleep whenever I get home, wake up in the late morning, and then spend some time volunteering at the church. I spend part of whatever's left of my time riding with Moose or my friends and occasionally some of the local hobby bikers. This area has some of the prettiest wilderness east of the Rockies, and it all looks great when you're zooming through on a bike.

That's my life now. Sure, it has its lonely spots, even though I have friends and Moose to help with that, but it's also got its own routine. There's no woman in my arms most nights, and no one who wants to stick around when there is.

I'm actually okay with that, though. Not because I don't want a good woman beside me—God knows I do after everything I've been through—but because my heart's already picked one. One I can't ever possibly have, but who I think about every night when I close my eyes.

As I shower in the tiny pod, I get my morning wood back just thinking about her: Julia, the preacher's daughter, and the brightest light in my life.

The church I volunteer at is one of three in town, and the only one liberal enough for me to tolerate, and traditional enough that they take feeding the hungry and tending the needy pretty damn seriously. Reverend Alderson, the stiff, but kind pastor in charge of the place, doesn't trust me too much. But he's still given me a chance to prove myself, and so I work hard on his food drives and repair program.

However, he would definitely draw the line at me trying to date his daughter. Pretty, sweet, and sexy young Julia Alderson is an angel, but she's barely old enough to drink—not that she ever would, I suspect. The girl has my heart—damn, she's had it for the past two years. But her father thinks I'm dangerous, and she's too young and too pure for me anyway.

She's little—barely comes up to my shoulder. She's got nearly a yard of soft auburn hair that she wears in a coiled braid when she's working, or in ringlets when she's feeling fancy. Modest, somber clothes barely do anything to conceal that robust young body of hers. And where her widower father's soft gray eyes are sad and tired, hers gleam brightly, full of life.

I know she likes me, too. We're buddies, working side-by-side at every church drive, chatting and laughing together. She likes my jokes. She loves my dog. And for some reason I can't fathom, she thinks I'm a great guy who just got a shitty break in life.

I've fallen so hard for her that I can't find my way back out to save my life. For two years now I've been her friend, worked with her to make Phoenicia better under her father's watchful and slightly suspicious eye, and closed my eyes every night wishing she was beside me. No matter who I'm with, she pops into my head when I get turned on, and I can't bust without thinking about her.

I open the trailer's tiny closet and look in on a mass of leather and denim. I grab a clean work shirt in black plaid from the drawers below then hunt up a clean pair of jeans and my vest. I pull it all on over my thermal long johns; it's maybe twenty degrees out.

Even Moose gets a vest before we go out: black leather lined in sheepskin, like mine. He whines when I put his paw covers on, putting up a little struggle that would flatten a smaller man.

"Oh, come on, don't be a damn baby about it, there's road salt everywhere," I grumble at him pointlessly as I finish dressing him and give him a belly scratch to calm him down.

Moose is a good dog. He even looks it, once you get past his size. He's as floppily enthusiastic as a puppy with his affection. He has a practically ear-to-ear doggie grin, and he's incredibly gentle around small people and other dogs. But of course he's going to cry a little about the weird doggie shoes that keep the salt and frost from his pads.

As soon as we step out of the trailer onto the thin crust of snow, the icy wind hits me like a slap in the face. "Damn!" I put my collar up and pull down my watch-cap with a sigh. The beauty of Upstate has a brutal side, but you either adapt or you get out.

Moose takes off like a shot across the field, chasing after one of the brave squirrels that's being blown around by the wind. The fat little guy runs up one of my maple trees and stops barely out of reach, barking and chattering. They all know Moose by now, and they know that the one unfortunate squirrel he actually caught only received a slobbery bath—and that Moose dropped it and ran after getting a bite on the nose.

It's hard to command fear and respect when even the squirrels know you melt in the face of cuteness.

I put my gloved hands on my hips and look around, the leather of my coat creaking slightly as I move. It still smells of the factory—like leather polish and lanolin from the sheepskin lining. The air has that particular dry-cold smell: sharp and almost dusty, tinged with woodsmoke.

My land is four acres and just across the creek from town. It's lightly sloped, and is ringed and dotted here and there with maples, black walnuts, apple trees, and an assortment of evergreens. The land is stony and overworked, and I've spent time digging out the rocks, planting clover, and plowing it under with borrowed gear, slowly building on it as I can afford to buy materials.

It isn't much to look at yet. The heavy duty fence is built from pallet wood and salvaged timber, bare now of its climbing vines, with a gate I built myself. The land is mostly bare, though I've started terracing the back half with bluestone I dug up. A salvaged stone path leads up to the trailer door.

Julia helped me lay the stones and gather moss to plant in between the cracks to keep out the cheatgrass. I told her she didn't have to, that she'd mess up her pretty little hands, but she just laughed and pulled on gloves. She's always trying to make me happy.

I wish she'd stop. It makes me love her more, and I can't touch her. In fact, if I ever so much as kiss her, I know I'd end up doing whatever she asks after that. And then we would both be in trouble.

She's twenty-one, hot and healthy. The way she looks at me sometimes makes me think I should get my eyes checked—those, or my head. It's gotta be wishful thinking on my part, believing that I see an expression on her face that suggests that she not only likes me, but...wants me.

Stop torturing yourself. I go to check my bikes. That damned drunk of a building inspector gave me hell about permits, so I had to buy a prefab shed for my vehicles and workshop. It's an ugly chunk of corrugated steel and plastic, and it sits on the windward side of the trailer. Most days it cuts the breeze and snow pile-up, but not today.

Today the winter wind is swirling, hitting from weird directions as it angles off the mountains. Sometimes it comes from the northeast, and it bites deep into my bones. There's definitely a storm coming. *I'd better get the spare propane tanks from the shed, in case I'm stuck inside for a while.*

I'm headed for the shed, just stepping onto the gravel driveway in front, when my phone buzzes in my pocket. "Huh." I check the time. It's seven in the morning, two days before Christmas. Who is even up this early?

Then I see the number and smile before I can stop myself and take the call. "Hey Jules, aren't you supposed to be sleeping?"

The voice on the other end is musical and full of excitement. "I can't! The food delivery's here early, and thank God, because they just upgraded the storm enough to give it a name. We have a damn blizzard headed this way just in time for Christmas!"

I stop dead. *Oh shit.* "Wait, wait, so we're doing deliveries today?"

"We are doing *everything* today. Sorting, bagging, delivery. They sent too much stuff, and if we don't get it distributed, it will go bad sitting inside."

The church had been approved for food distribution the same year that I fell in love with Julia. Three months later, the local eccentric, Dr. Whitman, donated enough scratch for us to expand the church basement and turn it into a food storage facility. It's pretty roomy, and stocked with enough stuff to cover the whole town for weeks if there was a disaster.

But the Reverend sees ongoing hunger as just as much of a disaster as a hurricane, and he's right. People—fucking *children*—go to bed hungry right here in my hometown and all around it, every day. I might be a bad guy, but even back in the big house a lot of guys wouldn't have liked that idea one bit. A lot of them went hungry as kids themselves.

My heart starts beating faster again, but this time it feels great. I'll have to shuffle some things around to spend my afternoon there as well, but I don't care. "Okay. What do you need from me?"

"You. The motorcycle with the sidecar. As many hours and as much gas as it takes." Her voice is so warm. I really can't stop smiling.

"Okay. I'll be over as soon as I can." I don't care if I go straight from there to work and fall into bed exhausted tomorrow morning. Spending the whole day with Julia makes the whole thing worth it.

I hang up and look over at Moose. "C'mon, boy, we got families to feed."

CHAPTER TWO

Julia

"There's no way that I can get a rental truck four days early, not this close to Christmas." Dad sits back from his laptop with a sigh, rubbing his lean face. He looks so crestfallen that I go over and hug him.

"Don't worry, Dad, I called ten volunteers while you were looking for one, and have them on standby. We've got one van, one pickup, seven cars, and Aaron's sidecar at our disposal." I deliberately use Aaron's first name, just to see that little twitch it puts in the corner of Dad's eye.

I love my Dad, and I've helped him run the church since Mom died. I look up to him in a lot of ways, but he has his flaws, just like everyone—the biggest one is that he prejudges people sometimes.

He's not racist, and he doesn't look down on the poor, but he makes certain judgments about bikers, stoners, hippies...guys with records. And the guy he's judged the most harshly is the one I want to spend my life with.

One day I hope to prove to him that he's got Aaron all wrong.

It hurts a little that he sticks to his prejudices toward the guy who has done so much heavy lifting around the church for years. Especially because Aaron is so important to me.

But all of that is secondary now compared to reassuring Dad that we're ready to get through this day. Twenty degrees? Icy? Hundreds of pounds of food to sort and distribute with a damn blizzard breathing down our necks?

No problem. We're on the case.

My dad blinks in surprise, and then smiles tentatively. "Good work," he says simply, and I hand him a fresh cup of coffee to fortify him for the day ahead.

After a quick breakfast of eggs, apple pancakes, and sausage, we're outside helping a small crowd of volunteers unload the delivery company's huge truck. I'm at one of the folding tables we have set up beside it, cutting open boxes of food and sorting the contents into smaller boxes to distribute.

The tables are wedged into the space between the delivery truck and the weathered side of the church, so that the heaving wind can't blow the lighter things away. We're hoping to eventually add a covered bay along the side to make unloading in extreme weather easier, but we can't quite get to that project yet. There are too many more important ones in the way.

The church is creaky and old, formerly a Dutch Reformed church that was sold after Hurricane Irene flooded so much of the area. A lot of people moved out of town after that. We moved in, and fixing and updating the big wooden building is as much a part of our lives as ministry or charity.

That's actually how I met Aaron Gates, former biker, current bouncer, handyman, dog daddy, and the man of my dreams. He is a guy who has spent a third of his life in jail or on parole for a crime he didn't commit, all so his brother wouldn't have to be put away for even longer. Now, he keeps drunks from acting up in town by night, and helps us with our church projects by day.

I remember the day I met him, over two years ago. He was new in town, and my father, who believes in second chances, as long as they don't involve dating his daughter, apparently, offered him a place in the congregation. Soon after that he started volunteering, and that was how I first crossed paths with him—him carrying lumber up to the steeple to reinforce it from within.

He's a mountain of a man. Big, burly, solid—he towers over everyone I know, even my dad, who is a beanpole. He's actually the exact opposite of my dad, appearance-wise—a little scruffy, with keen dark eyes, and short hair that almost looks black and is constantly swept back. When I saw him stomp past, whistling with what looked like an entire tree's worth of lumber on one muscled shoulder, everything stopped inside me, and all I could do was stare.

I don't really date. There isn't much opportunity—I don't have much time between church, volunteering, and commuting to and from seminary in Rochester, where I live for half the week during the semester. But every time I'm home and even remotely near Aaron, he's always in my thoughts.

Who would be better to spend the rest of my life with than my best buddy, the guy who gets things done, the guy to whom I can tell any secret and know that he will keep it? Yes, he's a lot older than I am, and there are some people in town who will never trust him—but I do. And I wish Dad did.

I get working as soon as I leave my dad, distributing frozen chickens into boxes—three to a box, along with a package of frozen ground beef. The vegetarians get beans, tofu, nuts, wild rice mixes, squash, and a couple of those horrible fake turkey loaves that apparently taste a lot better than they look. As I empty each box, I set it aside, and the man himself lumbers out of the truck with another.

"So, how's it going?" Aaron asks with that tender-eyed smile as he sets the big box on the table with a soft thud.

I beam at him. "We have enough food to give everyone half again as much as last year, take care of a lot of drop-ins, and then fill up our larders, too. I don't know how Whitman did it all, but I'll take the early delivery if it means we can get it all out before the storm comes." I tend to chatter when I'm excited.

"Me too." Again, I see that brief flash of a grin—a pretty rare occurrence. Aaron does smile a lot, especially when he's with me —or with his dog, who is keeping some of the other volunteers' kids busy playing. But he lights up when he's around me. People have commented on it before.

My father has also commented on it, and not in a good way.

However, in my dad's head, I'll probably always be twelve years old, even after he's retired, and I've taken over ministry. Maybe he would keep any guy who looks at me like Aaron does under a microscope. I wouldn't know, because I don't notice other guys.

Not like this.

I've already decided to do something about this whole ridiculous "unresolved sexual tension" thing. Ridiculous because I'm an adult, we're both single, and we should really do something about this.

Once the boxes are loaded up and closed, they go on a hand truck out to the volunteers' vehicles. The first cars are already coming back from their first set of deliveries, but Aaron has been stuck here, transferring cases of food and helping the less capable volunteers push their assigned hand trucks.

I love watching him work. The man is tireless. I can only imagine what he would be like in bed—not that I know much about that sort of thing, but hey, a girl can dream.

I'm catching myself staring at his ass for the third time when Marion, one of my volunteers, comes up to me, brushing snow off her rust-colored parka. She's a tall older woman with a long, strong-jawed face, and she smiles awkwardly at me. "Hey."

"Hi, Marion, what's going on?" I rearrange the contents of one of the boxes, making sure the loaves of bread don't get squashed, then fold it shut as I look up at her.

"A bit of odd news, actually. I'm just trying to find out who knows what. Did you hear about the mistletoe? Someone put it up all over town." Her lips twitch with a mix of amusement and baffled curiosity.

I blink at her slowly. "I've been here sorting chickens and canned goods since about eight. I haven't heard anything about this." *What exactly did I miss?*

"Mistletoe?" Aaron frowns as he brings coffee over in two plain white mugs. He hands me one, looks at Marion, who has clearly been out in the weather, and hands his over to her without missing a beat.

"Thank you." She warms her long fingers around the mug—not even the thickest gloves will keep out the biting cold if you're out there long enough. "Yes, the town's thick with it. Looks like some kind of prank. I guess the church didn't get hit?"

"Not as far as I know," I venture.

"That's because I took all those ridiculous sprigs down," my father sighs as he comes out, entering distribution figures into a spreadsheet on his laptop. "This morning, seven sharp, on my morning walk. I'm all for a good prank, but this is still God's house."

"I guess so, Reverend." Marion takes a deep swallow of her coffee while Aaron patiently turns to get himself and my Dad some more from inside. "Seems pretty strange, though. I wonder who would do something like that?"

My dad folds his arms, a faint, disinterested smile on his face. "I have no idea."

"You're no fun, Dad," I tease him once Marion goes back with her arms full, ready to start loading up her car again.

He eyes me. "Don't tell me you were in on this mistletoe prank. Apparently they're hanging everywhere in town."

I need to invite Aaron into town. "Uh, no, this is actually the first that I have heard of it. I'm kind of wondering who did it."

There are some really fun weirdos in Phoenicia. Most of them were either priced out of Woodstock, got sick of New York City, or seem to have just sprouted up here, like Dr. Whitman's son, Jack. Now that guy is definitely my number one suspect for a Christmas-themed prank like this.

After all, every year starting mid-December, his Dad's lawn looks like the Macy's Christmas Parade, and his family throws a Christmas feast for the whole town and makes huge food donations. Jack was raised in a family that loves Christmas.

Jack—who is sexy but can't hold a candle to Aaron—is the fun kind of idle rich. He's a skier with a rack of trophies, known for following the snow season across the equator to Australia, just so he can enjoy it longer. The half of the year that he's here, he parties and flirts his way through the mountains. Then, as soon as the snow melts, he's gone again.

He has the time, cash, and energy to double his father's food donation early—and yet, right on time. He has just the kind of odd sense of humor, paired with a huge list of friends and the connections necessary, to see that our morning food distribution wakes up everyone early so they'll have to witness the prank—his prank? —in town. The big weirdo may also have the world's only bulk mistletoe hook-up—he probably got a reference from his father.

I have to hand it to the both of them about the donation part, at least. Most rich New Yorkers are alarmingly self-interested. But not those two. They're going above and beyond to spread the Christmas cheer—and maybe some kisses—this year.

I turn to eye Aaron speculatively as he comes back out with mugs of coffee in each fist. He hands one to my father, who thanks him a little stiffly, and then comes over to me...slowing down with a look of mild worry on his face. "What?"

I smile with all the innocence. "Nothing."

CHAPTER THREE

Aaron

Sweet little Julia is up to something, I can just tell. She's smiling too much, and she's looking at me with this mischievous expression that leaves me just a bit concerned.

Julia doesn't know how to flirt, and I thank God for that, because if she ever really came on to me, she would have me wrapped around her little finger in an instant. Hell, I'd be happy about it.

Her father, on the other hand, would probably drive me out of the church like I fucked the Virgin Mary. And besides, there's one thing about me that he's right about: I don't deserve someone as pure and hot and full of life as Julia. If she thinks that I do, she's selling herself short.

. . .

But a guy can dream, right? As long as I remember that *all* I'm gonna be doing is dreaming.

We make it to one in the afternoon before we run into our first glitch, which is amazing given the huge amount of food we have to sort and pass out in a short time. But when things finally go wrong, they do it in a big way.

"What do you mean, we've lost track? How much food got loaded downstairs?" Poor Reverend Alderson is managing to keep his voice quiet, but his eyes show that he's ready to tear out his own hair. *Poor guy.* He might have a stick up his ass, but he doesn't deserve stress in return for his kindness.

Julia and I exchange glances and she gives me a nod. We both hover around while the crisis unfolds, ready to step in.

The bearer of bad news is Tomxmy, a kid who works at the gas station. He's a little bear of a guy in Coke-bottle glasses, who squirms at the note of desperation in the Reverend's voice. "Um, well...enough that we're having trouble opening the doors."

"But we haven't even finished unloading the truck...?" He looks into the back of the delivery truck, from which boxes are still coming out, and over at all the volunteers' cars, which have all done at least three trips around the county and are loaded to the gills again. "How did they fit it all? I can't believe I'm saying this, but this is almost too much of a good thing!"

. . .

"Don't worry, Dad," Julia speaks up, walking over and offering to take his laptop. "I'll go down to the storeroom and tally things up. I'll just need some help getting the door open."

He relinquishes the laptop. "You're sure? I have no idea what it's like down there right now—it might be a total mess."

"I'll manage." She looks over at me. "C'mon, I may need some help shuffling some of the stacks of boxes around. The truck's almost empty. Everyone else can take it from here."

I nod and trail her inside, trying not to walk too close. Too much of that, and I know I'll be in trouble again. I can't be of use with the food distribution if I'm stumbling around with boner-brain.

"You know, I know it's stressing Dad, but having so much donated food that we lose track of it all is a pretty good inconvenience." We head through the kitchen and into the hallway, which is narrow and floored with peeling linoleum. I mentally add that to my repair list.

I nod agreement as we head for the freight elevator at the end of the hall. Too many times, especially these days, food drives scratch along on almost nothing. "You said it. But directing the whole event still has to be stressful for him."

"Always. He's too rigid and stuck in routines for his own good—

big changes always stress him out." She stops in front of the elevator and I pull the lever, unlatching the pull-down safety gate and shoving it upward. She ducks in ahead of me. "Thank you, sir."

"You're welcome, ma'am." There's that smile I can't fight again.

The elevator's roomy and dim, with a high ceiling. There's an odd, spicy green smell hanging around the air in the place. It's a little familiar, but I can't place it. Has someone donated a bunch of mustard greens to go with the other stuff in the fridges downstairs?

On her way in, Julia pauses for just a moment, and I hear her let out a little laugh before she continues inside, as if she's just thought of something—or noticed something. I step in after her and close the gate. "So," she says suddenly as I'm reaching to throw the lever and send us down, "you know all that mistletoe Dad says he removed from the church?"

I pause, the naughty tone in her voice startling me, and look back at her. "Yeah?"

She reaches past me and pulls the lever, closing the door on us and sending the elevator rumbling slowly downward. "He missed a sprig."

I look down at her and see her wide grin as she steps closer...and then look up, straight at a bundle of mistletoe hanging right above me. *Crap.*

I FREEZE, knowing what is about to happen and almost dreading it, knowing as well that I can't stop her—I don't want to. She presses her body into me, the pleasure of it mixing with a searing hunger as I fight not to grab hold of her. Her lips brush against mine and her arms slip around my neck as she clings to me.

SHE KISSES me with a mix of sensuality and tenderness that melts my heart and brings my cock fully awake in seconds. Aching, I groan against her mouth, feeling my whole body respond involuntarily while my free will floats away on a cloud of bliss.

HOLY SHIT. Oh my God. I'm in trouble.

I DON'T CARE.

WHY DID I ever hold back from kissing her? I have never felt anything so right in my life. It's sweeter than my first breath of free air.

I PULL HER CLOSER, feeling her squirm against me, her full breasts rubbing against my chest through her layers of clothing while her tongue teases its way into my mouth. I can hear the low, starved groans vibrating through my throat as I respond, a wave of sensual hunger running from my toes to the tip of my head.

I have to have her. Now. Right now.

Wait, what am I doing? I gently pull away, and she makes a small, disappointed noise in her throat.

When I finally get control of myself, I stare down at her in amazement. "Julia...what are you doing?"

"What I've wanted to do for more than a year," she replies with a wicked grin.

"Baby, we really shouldn't—" I start, and she simply moves closer, laying a slim, warm finger against my lips.

"Shhhh."

I'm doomed.

The elevator rattles to a stop, and we're kissing again, and we stand there wrapped up in each other for so long that I lose track of why we're down here. She's so soft, so warm...so fragrant. So perfect.

I try to be gentle. But again, she's not making it easy. She presses into me with the eager and slightly clumsy enthusiasm of someone totally new to kissing. The realization that she probably is—that I might be the first to ever feel her this way—only turns me on even more.

BUT THEN, before either of us can catch our breath or say anything about what has just happened, there's a heavy clunk, and the elevator starts rising again. *What?*

THE HAIRS on the back of my neck start prickling and I let her go, breathing hard, moving back against the wall of the elevator while she wipes her mouth and steps back as well. Someone's called the elevator and will be joining us in a moment.

THE OUTER DOOR rumbles up as we come to a stop, and my heart sinks into my boots. The Reverend's standing there, scowling at us both.

CHAPTER FOUR

Julia

The kiss was everything I had hoped for. Especially when I realized how enthusiastically Aaron was returning my kiss—he must have been crushing on me even harder than I was on him. I lied when I said that I had only wanted to kiss him for a year.

It's been over two years. Since the first day I saw him. I went to bed that night wondering what his mouth would taste like.

Now I know. He tastes like coffee and mint, and mixed with his warm, musky male scent in my nostrils, he's intoxicating. Knowing only makes me want more.

When he steps away from me I'm so dizzy and keyed up that his sudden absence against my body hurts like a missing limb. But a split second later, I realize that someone has called the elevator, and we are about to have company.

Crap. I wipe my mouth and move back against the wall, catching my breath. *I definitely need some real privacy before I try this mistletoe trick again.*

THE LAPTOP'S on the floor. I can't remember whether I set it there or dropped it, but I snatch it up and check it. No damage.

THEN THE GATE OPENS, and I see that it's Dad—standing there with his arms folded.

SHIT SHIT SHIT—

I GIVE HIM A SMILE. I'm not actually doing anything wrong, after all. But overprotective fathers have to be reassured sometimes. "Hi Dad! Did you forget something?"

"I THOUGHT I would come down here and help you tally," he replies after a moment of staring suspiciously at the two of us. I feel my heart clench—but after a few moments he relaxes and holds out his hand for his laptop. "If a room that large is full of supplies, then it's not a two-person job."

"That's true enough, Reverend," Aaron responds with a touch of relief in his eyes. For a moment, I feel guilty. But then I remember how he shook when I kissed him, and how his whole huge, solid body turned to putty in my hands.

. . .

Oh no. We're definitely not done with this. I smile to myself before looking up at my dad and nodding. "Let's get started, then."

Aaron and I settle back into our friendly rapport for the rest of the afternoon. By the end of it, we're stocked up, and so is everyone on our donation list. We're also both exhausted and sore.

"I gotta get a shower before my shift," Aaron groans, stretching and rolling his massive shoulders. For just a moment, he shoots me a smoldering glance, which tells me he wishes I would join him. But being Aaron, he's back to not saying a thing.

Probably because dear old Dad planted himself right beside us after he found us in the elevator, watching us both like a very irritated hawk in a clerical collar for the rest of the afternoon. Dad doesn't miss much. I know I'm in for a lecture when we get home. He's out of bounds, but I'll have to take it anyway, because he loves me, and he's too stressed right now for me to fight it.

But that kiss...it told me everything. I hadn't been deceiving myself. The guy I've been waiting for has been waiting for me, too. My dad will have to find a way to cope with that eventually. I just don't want him to deal with it now.

I also don't want to deal with him dealing with it now. I can only imagine the tidal wave of drama that will be set loose once I finally tell him my intentions—to be with Aaron forever... It's the damn holidays. I'm tired, I'm in love, and I want to be happy. I also want Dad to be happy.

Sometimes, ignorance is bliss.

Unfortunately, he's already suspecting something. When I finally get home, shower, and get into my purple sweatpants and a giant, pink flannel shirt, he's very quiet as he heats up the lasagna I fixed for tonight.

He hasn't turned on his jazz station. That's a huge red flag—I'm definitely in for a lecture.

I come down the narrow stairs with a little sigh, looking out each of the little windows lining the stairway as I pass them. Our house sits behind the church, a tall, slim Victorian half hidden in the trees. Like a lot of buildings up here, it's painted white with green trim and a red door. Unlike a lot of buildings up here, it's surrounded by gravestones from the churchyard.

It makes for an interesting view as the sun sets and the snowflakes swirl down. Just that *Nightmare Before Christmas* touch that I like best.

I prepare myself mentally as I walk. All my life, Dad's been overprotective of me. But once we lost Mom, he got...brittle.

. . .

Before then, his portrayal of the stick-up-the-ass minister had a humorous edge that was gentled by my Mom's presence. But now, it's like part of him has frozen over, making him cold and stiff, and too easy to snap. I handle him carefully, not just because I hate the drama, but because I realize that these days, drama's really not good for him.

I wish Mom was here.

Mom would have loved Aaron. Her dad used to be a Hells Angel before he settled down and started his own motorcycle garage back in California. Grandpa took me riding a few times when I was tiny, and I remember Mom laughing as I squealed with delight, while at the same time, Dad fluttered his hands slightly and made small, nervous protests.

I've always wished that I could run off on some adventure on a motorcycle, like Mom once did, before I'd have to do the responsible thing and settle in for church duties and seminary. But losing Mom meant that someone had to step in and help Dad, at least part time. That's what I do now, when I'm in town, and over the phone or online when I'm in Buffalo.

It's good practice for the job I want: taking over this place and letting my Dad enjoy his retirement. He'll still volunteer his head off, of course. But once I'm the one wearing the collar around here, I can shoo him off to his books and jazz when he gets too overwhelmed.

· · ·

DAD KNOWS I'm an adult and has seen what I can do, but he just can't back off with his hovering and protectiveness. I know why, so I don't normally complain much.

HIS HEAD'S still full of nightmares over Mom's loss. He's scared to lose me, too. Of course, I understand.

BUT SOMETIMES, trying to fight against his overprotective fears makes me crazy with frustration. Thus, I take a couple of minutes to focus myself before joining him in the dining room.

"YOU DID GOOD WORK TODAY," he starts off, as I settle into my seat across from his. Dad always starts and ends serious discussions with the positive, so we start with our ears open and end without wanting to keep yelling at each other.

"IT NEEDED TO BE DONE. Besides, it was just amazing. Everyone's fridge will be full well before the storm."
I move our entree in front of me and set to work with a knife and spatula. He'd set out the lasagna in its baking dish, like a giant TV dinner. At least he remembered a trivet.

HE NODS MUTELY and just watches for a minute as I cut generous squares of lasagna for each of our plates. It's a one-dish meal, full of beef, cheese, spinach, mushrooms, homemade red sauce, and spices. I cook for fun, and to see the way the men in my life light up when I set a good meal in front of them.

. . .

"You okay, Dad?" I ask him gently as he sits stiffly at his seat instead of starting prayer.

"I'm worried about you, Julia," he says very gently, and my smile freezes on my face.

Here we go. "Okay, what's got you worried? I told you I'll start saving for the four wheel drive instead of that cute Kia. You're right, commuting to and from Buffalo in winter isn't safe in a small city car."

He blinks and sits back slightly. "Wait, you did? I was...very tired this morning."

I nod. "That's okay, maybe I wasn't clear." It's always best to pretend obliviousness to derail suspicion. Also, he *is* right about the damn car.

He nods briefly, seeming just a touch more relaxed. At least he can see that I still have my common sense. "Good. But—no, that isn't what's worrying me. I knew you'd make the right decision about trading in your truck."

"Okay, so, what's the concern?" I look down at my plate. My mouth is watering. We don't take a single bite before prayers in this house, which means I either have to resolve his worries quickly, or let my lasagna go cold.

. . .

"You and Mr. Gates. I'm concerned about his influence on you." He watches my face.

"This may be the twelfth time in two years that you've said that, Dad, and in that time, Aaron hasn't been a bad influence on me. If anything, we've been a good influence on him." And Aaron has come back strong. I remember a time when getting him to smile or make eye contact was a Herculean task.

My father rubs his face and then looks up at me, his eyes a little bleary from exhaustion and frustration. "That's very likely true. I'm not discounting the improved state of Mr. Gates's soul, which has been remarkable. He does a great deal of good work for us, and since he's gotten back on his feet, he has asked for little in return."

"Then what's the issue? Seriously, Dad, you keep coming back to this, and then nothing ever happens to make us regret my friendship with him." I am trying to point out the history of his suspicions and all the times he's cried wolf about Aaron.

"The guy cares about me. About you too, for that matter," I add.

"That's different." He looks away. "I just don't want you getting hurt."

. . .

"Why do you think he would hurt me?" I'm genuinely astonished.

"Julia, he may care about you, but he has a history of violence. He was in jail for ten years for beating a man nearly to death. What if he can't leave that violence behind?"

"He has. Dad...I've told you that he went to jail in his brother's place. He's innocent."

"If he's innocent, he would have fought for his freedom and his reputation. He tells a story about taking the fall for his older brother, but how believable is that?" His frown doesn't waver. He's genuinely worried, and I'm not quite sure how to reassure him.

"Dad, this is a guy who gives all his weekends to us, provides the town with thousands of dollars of free labor every year, and has worked like crazy to leave his old life behind. He makes big sacrifices for others all the time—and for his brother. I believe him, Dad, and I think that time will prove me right."

He winces and looks away, his expression so troubled that I fall silent. "You're in love with him," he says very quietly. "And so you're defending him. Just like your mother did with her father during his hell-raising days." His eyes rise to mine slowly. "Did you think I wouldn't notice?"

"Dad, look." My heart is banging away and sending ice water rushing through my veins. *Oh God, please help me out here, I'm trying to ease his fears without treating him like a child.* "First and most importantly, it isn't that I thought you would not notice anything. It's that I thought you would trust me to show good judgment, and to know that if I trust Aaron enough to want him in my life, there are good reasons for that."

That catches him by surprise, and he relaxes a little more, taking a deep breath. "You're concerned that I'm worried because I'm not in full possession of the facts?"

"I think that's part of it." But my Dad doesn't want or need to be in full possession of the facts, not if some of them are nonessential and would hurt his peace of mind.

Aaron didn't influence me to kiss him. He didn't push a kiss on me. I kissed him under the damn mistletoe, and I have no regrets. But it would still freak my Dad out to learn about it.

"Fine. What facts am I not aware of?" He looks down at the cooling lasagna and sighs. "Briefly."

"The one you should most know is that he's anything but violent, Dad. Go into the bar some time while he's working, and you'll see it in action. He has a job that could be violent if he made it so—he has drunks from three counties testing his patience all night."

THAT CATCHES HIS INTEREST. He nods, brow furrowing. "Go on."

"HE HAS NEVER RAISED a hand to any of them. He's trained in judo and just marches them outside; sometimes he even holds them for Earl when the cops need to be called. Nobody has ever complained of rough treatment except for one guy who Aaron pulled off a woman who was calling for help." These things are important. All of them.

"DAD, I'm not asking you to take me at my word. I'm asking you to look at the man that Aaron is, the man he proves himself to be every day. Even if he was a bad man once, he's done his penance, and he's been seeking redemption. He's also a really responsible guy." This is going better than expected, but I still wish I could plow through and soothe myself with too much lasagna.

"HE'S OLD FOR YOU." That protest is a bit weaker.

"HE IS." I run into a wall for a moment. *Come on, come on, you were doing so well a moment ago.* "But I want the kind of guy who is stable, responsible, wants to get serious, and has his own money. And I'm sorry, but have you *met* guys my age?"

COLLEGE-AGE GUYS often appear to be exactly the kind of people my father and I despise: horny, faithless, thoughtless, and often, seemingly brainless. Maybe I just have incredibly bad luck, but I keep running into guys my age who seem bent on fucking the ministry student like it's a personal challenge—with no other interest in me at all.

He lets out a soft laugh. "Sadly yes. I was one. You have a point. I just...worry. I admit I'd prefer you settle down with someone who lives here rather than someone over in Buffalo. There...isn't someone else in Buffalo, is there?"

I roll my eyes. "Dad! We wouldn't be having this conversation if there were someone in Buffalo!"

He relaxes more, and even lets out a little laugh. "I'm sorry. I just don't want you making any decisions you might end up regretting."

"But Dad," I say patiently, "everyone has regrets sometimes. I know life's full of trials and disappointments, and I need you to trust me to be tough enough to handle it. Okay?"

He smiles faintly. "Okay." But then he frowns, half-theatrically. "But don't let me catch you kissing that biker!"

"Dad, if you catch me kissing that biker, there will be mistletoe involved." *Because from now on, we're doing our kissing in private.*

. . .

He folds his arms. "All the more reason for me to pull down every sprig of the stuff I see."

"Humph," my only response. But at least he's satisfied enough by my answers to say prayers and let us eat.

We both go down for a nap after our very early dinner. Dad has to take some of his sinus meds and ends up conked out for good. I feel bad for him...except that it means he won't wake up for at least eight hours.

I can do a lot in eight hours.

I dress very carefully—I don't want to look too obvious, with too much makeup or fancy hair. I don't want there to be any chance of gossip when I'm seen around Aaron.

The warm, sheepskin lining of my coat rubs softly against my skin, teasing me as I think about his hands on me. The thermal bottoms are a little scratchy, especially where they tuck into my snow boots, and so is the simple blue wool scarf I tuck into my collar at my throat.

They do the job, though. When I finally walk outside, the cold doesn't get through, despite my...modified...outfit. *If Dad knew what I was doing he would flip. But the thing that would make him flip the most is that I'm the one on a mission.*

I leave the lights on and bring my phone, pretending that I'm going out on an errand. If Dad wakes up unexpectedly, that's what I'll tell him. We're out of eggnog anyway.

The snow has stopped again, leaving a thin icy crust on the sidewalks. It's such a short walk to the gas station convenience store and the bar across from it that I can excuse going out without my truck and being in the area. From there, it's a short walk up the hill to Aaron's land.

And his trailer. And his bed.

I've never felt like this before in my life. I know it's because of him. That first kiss was off-the-scales awesome—definitely worth the wait. But now that I've had a taste of him, I don't want to wait any more.

5

CHAPTER FIVE

Aaron

I know I'm in for a really shitty shift when I come in and hear a familiar voice yell, "Hey, Lucky!" from the corner of the bar.

I stop dead, squeezing my eyes shut, the euphoria from that kiss with Julia vanishing like smoke. There's only one guy around anymore who calls me that, and I never wanted to hear from him again.

I open my eyes and look over to the voice, and see my big brother Daniel leaning toward me from his seat at a corner table. Older by almost twenty years, with gray in his hair, but with the same dress and manner that I remember. He's grinning wide enough for the scar on his cheek to crease like a bad seam in his leathery skin. *Not again.*

"Give me a sec." I send a beer over to him to mollify his alcoholic ass, then check in with my boss, Eddy, who nods at me and twitches a small smile as I approach. "Hey, I'm in for the night. Any problems? Like with him?"

We both look over at Daniel, who is still grinning—obviously drunk—his face red beneath the road tan and his overlong curls sticking wetly to his forehead. He looks like me if I was a foot shorter, ate nothing but cheeseburgers and booze, and got beat a few times with the ugly stick.

He's also an asshole. But he's family, and he knows I make sacrifices for my loved ones. So the first thing I wonder is what he's here to ask me for, and how much trouble he plans to cause until he gets it.

"That guy? No problem, except he should probably be cut off about now. He's kind of a jackass, but I saw the resemblance, so we didn't throw him out." My boss offers a lopsided smile.

"I wouldn't have taken it personally if you had thrown him out," I admit. "I'll go deal with him. Yell if you need me."

He nods, likely knowing it wouldn't be necessary. Being in prison has left me with an instinct for trouble. Even if Daniel wasn't my brother, I would still be keeping a closer eye on him than on anyone else in here, for just that reason.

He's smirking as I walk over. It's all I can do not to grab him by the collar and haul him off his feet—and as he sees the look in my eyes, the smirk fades. "Hey," he says in that used-car salesman tone that he uses when he wants to talk me into something. I'd hoped never to hear it again.

"What the hell are you doing here, Daniel?" I demand in a low, hard tone as I walk up to him.

In response, he pushes out the chair across the table from him with his foot. "Just a little talk."

I take a deep breath. Eddy's watching us like a hawk between serving drinks, in case I need backup. I need to keep this job. I smile tightly, settle into the seat and then say, "We shouldn't be having a conversation at all."

He chuckles. "I'm hurt. Yeah, yeah, I know, you said after everything you did for me, you wanted out of the business and me out of your life. I get it, I do, and I know you're a stand-up guy. Not every guy will do a dime and change for his brother."

I stare at him. "The deal was, I do that for you, and then you walk out of my life and take the gang and all your crazy baggage with it. The drugs, the guns, everything you dragged me into when I was fifteen and too dumb to know better."

"Oh yeah, I get it, I do. And you got a pretty raw deal in prison, or so I hear. Only got one working kidney left, isn't that right?" His voice has a wheedling tone of mock sympathy to it.

"Yeah, that's right." I lean forward, knowing three things: I'm bigger, fitter, and tougher than him; he's on my turf and drunk as hell; and he owes me way, way too much to be coming back for another favor now. "Now, once again, why the fuck are you bothering me? Are you dying? Is Dad dying?"

"I don't know. Old bastard doesn't talk to me anymore." He shrugs nonchalantly and takes a deep swallow of his beer. "And I know he hangs up every time you try to call. Doesn't he?"

My mouth works and I look away. He's right on the nose. Dad married his high school sweetheart, went to church every Sunday and broke his back at a construction job. He taught me joinery, how to carve a chain from a stick of wood, and how to frame a shed.

He's career military, retired now. A patriot. A good man. He doesn't deserve two trouble-making sons, both of whom are convicted felons now.

He used to think I was a good man. But when I went down for Daniel after he beat the hell out of that banker, Dad didn't care that they had the wrong brother. After all, I didn't fight it.

He never once called me when I was in jail or on probation, and after enough hang-ups, I gave up on calling him.

"Wow, that really did hit a nerve, didn't it?" Daniel tugs on his pointed chin, his eyes full of sly mockery. "So I was right."

"I don't know if he'd talk to me if I called him now. I haven't tried in years." I keep my voice neutral, ignoring the gutted feeling that thinking about Dad always leaves me with.

That seems to surprise him. "Thought you planned to go legit after we parted ways, get back in his good graces."

"There's no getting back in Dad's good graces after all the trouble you dragged me into." I blame Daniel for about eighty percent of it anyway. I could have said no. I could have run, could've let Daniel and the Laughing Boys hunt me. I could even have fought back and gotten my ass beat.

"No, probably not," he replies thoughtfully. "But that cat's been out of the bag for a while, hasn't it?"

"Just fucking spit it out, Daniel. Why are you here?" It occurs to me that if I grab the son of a bitch, bash his head against the table a few times, drag him across the floor by one leg and pitch him out into the snow, everyone else here would simply ask me what he did. But I don't. I'm just not that guy any more.

"I'm here to take you back with me," he replies simply.

I stare at him. *Balls.* But that's Daniel—all balls, no sense, and absolutely no honor. I thought he had disappointed me for the last time when he left me to rot in jail without paying my bail and fines. It seems I was wrong. "No."

He cocks his head. "Wait, did you just tell me no? Do you have any fucking idea who you're dealing with here, baby brother?"

I push my chair back and stand, stepping around the table, looming over him. He hasn't seen me since I was that scared kid headed into jail. He has no idea what the past eighteen years have done to me—I was thrown into the pit and I climbed back out with my fingernails. That changes a man. "Do you?" I ask him softly.

It slowly seems to dawn on him that things have changed a bit. His eyes widen, and he goes quiet for a moment before smiling up at me. "You're right, I do owe you big. And normally, I would leave you alone just like you want. But I need you down south, baby brother."

I shake my head. "No deal. I've got a life here now. I am not giving it up to follow you into the mouth of Hell again."

He starts to argue—and then his head snaps around to focus on the door as it opens, the bell on it ringing. His eyebrows go up, and I quickly turn to look.

Oh shit.

It's Julia. Beautiful, sweet Julia, bundled in her one good coat, a scarf covering her hair and throat and tucked into her collar. She looks around for me, and I wince. *Crap. Not now. Not while Daniel is here!*

She sees me and her face lights up; she takes a step in my direction, and then her face falls in confusion as she catches sight of Daniel. Quickly she goes to the bar instead, and I let out a small sigh of relief. I'll deal with her after I deal with my brother. *I just hope he hasn't noticed that—*

"Friend of yours?" he asks almost teasingly.

Shit.

"Well, well! Cute little piece of ass! What is she, twenty? No wonder you don't want to leave!" He gets up and starts sauntering past me, headed straight for Julia.

I grab him by the arm and just stand there solidly. He stops short—and the sudden realization that he can't move past me or pull his arm free shocks his attention away from Julia. I look past him; she is watching us with a worried expression.

"What?" he demands, getting a little loud. "I just want to introduce myself."

"You are drunk and an asshole. She's a nice girl who doesn't need your kind of problems anywhere near her. Leave her alone." My voice drops to a growl at the last, and he gives me a shocked look.

"Holy shit, you really must like this piece of tail." He moves back to his chair. I let him go and he sits down. "Who is she?"

"None of your damn business."

He laughs. "You know I'm gonna find out."

My blood runs cold at his threat, and I lean down into his face. "What you're gonna do is go the fuck back to New Orleans and leave me alone. I already did more for you than you ever deserved, just so they wouldn't lock you up and throw away the key. That was the last thing I'm ever doing for you."

His smirk fades. "I'm in serious need here."

"I was in serious need when I ended up in the system without anyone to visit me or throw me a lifeline. Nobody in the club, none of my family—not one of you so much as sent me a damn Christmas card."

"You want me to get you a Christmas card? Is that what this is about?" His drunken bravado sets my teeth on edge.

"This is about you leaving." I rub the bridge of my nose. "I gave you most of my life, Daniel, between the club and what happened. I'm done with that. You gonna shoot me for that, like you used to threaten? Go right ahead."

He gives me a mock look of shock. "I wouldn't dream of harming my own brother, even if he is being a giant ungrateful fuck who forgets who practically raised him."

"You get my point. Just go, Daniel. You're not wanted here."

He scoffs and stands, doing his best to stare me in the eyes. "So that's it, huh? You want me to do this the hard way? Because I can still do that. You talk about how you've built a life here? Well, that's fine. Maybe I'll just destroy every part of it, and then you won't have anything tying you here."

There's ice in my veins now. My hands clench at my sides. "You can try," I growl back. "But you'll fail. And it'll cost you."

He starts heading for the door—with me following right

behind him—laughing hollowly the whole way. "We'll see," he replies, and looks back at Julia one last time before I practically shove him out the door.

CHAPTER SIX

Julia

"I don't understand," I say to Aaron. My heart hurts, and the lambskin lining of my coat is scratchy against my back. I feel vulnerable and a little sick from watching the bizarre exchange between him and the other biker. *Someone from his past?* "You want me to leave?"

Every time that man looked over at me and smirked, I felt a chill run down my back that made me pull my coat around me closer, like a layer of armor. I didn't feel comfortable with him here, with the way he was talking to Aaron, or with the way Aaron reacted. I smelled trouble on that man, thick as body odor and beer fumes.

Fortunately, he was only around for about five minutes before Aaron basically escorted him out the door. I sigh with relief once the door closes behind him—but it catches in my throat as I see the man walk over to one of the frosted windows and stand there outside, trying to peer in.

Aaron comes over and tells me that I should leave. And I protest, of course. He doesn't seem to know what to say. "Look," he starts, then coughs into his fist and glances at the window. "Things just got complicated."

"I thought they were already complicated," I say quietly as the bartender brings me my Irish coffee.

"They are. But God knows I don't want you caught up in any of what just went on, so we're probably going to have to take a break from each other for a while. I'll try to still be around the church to help out and stuff, but we shouldn't...associate." He speaks so reluctantly that my heartache eases a little.

"How long?" I ask in a pained tone, and his hand brushes mine, maybe on instinct.

"Just a few days. We probably need to cool off anyway." Another regretful look. "But you already know that."

"No, I don't." I've never felt so sure about anything in my life. "No regrets about this afternoon, Aaron. None."

He sighs through his nose and nods. "You're really selling yourself short, sweetheart. I'm trouble. I don't mean to be, but it follows me around."

Now I just want to hug him even more than I usually do. He's always the one to sacrifice for others. But I won't let him do it this time. "Who is that man?"

"That's Daniel," he replies in a falsely light tone, looking over at the window again. The man's creepy silhouette still stands there, his breath wearing through the frost. "That's my brother."

My eyes widen. *Oh shit.* He's warned me about his brother before.

Aaron has told me a lot about himself, probably more than anyone else in town. It started back when he was drinking more and had just started to realize that he could tell me anything: the gang he was pulled into too young, the crimes he witnessed and had to play lookout for, Daniel's impulsiveness and violence.

He told me about the day his brother beat a bank executive

into a coma because the poor man panicked during a robbery and couldn't remember the safe combination. Daniel, who owed crippling debts to some terrifying people, flew into a rage out of desperation. Only Aaron restraining him had stopped Daniel from committing murder.

The man, addled by terror and an anxiety disorder, got the two brothers mixed up in the line-up, insisting that Aaron attacked him. The police detective had refused to believe it; he had noticed Daniel's criminal record, and Aaron's lack of one.

Aaron took the fall anyway. He told me that he did it because Daniel was two felonies in and was about to get life in prison without parole. I cried when I found out.

"Why is he here?" I ask incredulously, keeping my voice low.

"He wants to take me back to New Orleans with him." He scratched his check, rubbing at his five o'clock shadow as his lips twisted in disgust. "Back to the club. For keeps."

"How did they end up in New Orleans?" I feel like I'm a step behind suddenly. I know I have no business expecting him to tell me every damn thing, but something crazy is going on, and I need help sorting it out in my head.

The bartender brings him a single shot of whiskey and he swallows it down like medicine. "Daniel and the Laughing Boys couldn't hack it in the Northeast. So he led all five of the remaining members down the coast to the Big Easy three years ago. I only found out about it through one of the guys that left the club."

"And now they're having trouble in New Orleans, and he wants your help." *No, absolutely not. There is no way I am putting up with him being dragged away when he's just starting to be happy again. Not when we're right on the brink of being together.*

"That's pretty much it." He gets a regular coffee as his next drink. He's on duty after all, and I know that for him only the coffee is free.

"My brother knew where to look. I grew up here, after all. So, did he. Difference is I always wanted to come back to Phoenicia, and I made the mistake of admitting that."

"We have to get him away from here." I want to cry at the thought of Aaron leaving—and it makes me want beat this guy's ass. But of course, I'm not really the type to do either. I would rather find some sane way of fixing the problem.

"You just let me take care of this situation, sweetheart. He's a drunk, he's violent, and he's not used to New York winters anymore. I don't think he'll be able to keep out of trouble, and I don't want you anywhere near him." His hand covers mine briefly, comfortingly.

It makes me want to take him by the hand and lead him outside and down the street to his trailer. But he's at work, and I know I have to be patient.

I suddenly feel stupid. He won't be free for hours, but when I left home all I was thinking about was what I would do to him once he was done work. Maybe he's right, and I'm too damned young to be out here like this.

And if I had not come, that creep would not know my face now, or know that I'm associated with Aaron, and that will probably cause even more issues for Aaron. He is already talking about a cooling-off period, even if it's short.

"What can I do?" I ask him softly, brushing his fingers with mine.

"Don't let him get near you. Don't let him follow you home. Do you have your truck?" His voice sounds harsh, full of worry. I blush.

"I walked down. It was almost clear out and I was stiff from earlier so I needed it." *Crap. I really am naive sometimes.* Though really, how could I have anticipated that a dangerous scumbag from his past would be here?

"Shit. Okay. Can you get a friend to take you back?" He

glances at the window again. Daniel is pacing slowly, hands behind back. My stomach flips and I nod. "Good. I can't leave my post and take you back home right now."

"Okay." My heart's in my boots now. *Stupid.* "I just wanted to see you."

His smile looks too forced for my comfort. "Normally that wouldn't be a problem. But there's just too much going on. With you, with this." He looks so tired. "I've gotta finish my shift without anything else crazy happening."

"I understand. I'll just stay right here until my ride picks me up." I swallow a lump in my throat and cover my unhappy look with a big gulp of coffee.

He touches my back, leaving a tingling spot in its wake. "Thanks, sweetheart. I'll catch up with you as soon as I can."

He leaves me as I start looking through my phone to see what friends in town would still be up after nine, and I'm fighting tears. This isn't how things were supposed to go.

There's only one thing in this world that I want just for me, and that's him. Cute cars, a rich lifestyle, and some boyfriend thrown at me by my father with his stamp of approval are all luxuries that I can live without. But more and more, it feels like I just can't live without Aaron.

I'm starting on my second cup of coffee when the door opens, making me jump. It's not Daniel, though, but chubby, lovable Dr. Whitman, decked out in a forest green coat. He smiles at me warmly as he approaches, and stops by the bar stool that Daniel vacated. "Is this seat taken?"

"It is now." I have to force my smile as he settles onto it. "How are you doing, Doctor?"

"I'm doing well, though I think I should warn you that it is going to be quite a snowy Christmas." He winks. "But at least less people will be going hungry and cold than before."

"Yeah, about that," I venture carefully, grateful for the

sudden and important distraction. "Do you have any idea how much the company you hired actually sent over?"

I still can't quite believe that anyone wealthy would be so generous without any encouragement. I've never seen it before, except with the Whitmans. But perhaps that's part of what makes them special.

His smile becomes part wince. "As I understand it, they were both early and generous. I apologize about the early part. I let my son make the arrangements this year, and he's always been a touch...mischievous."

I nod slowly, feeling vindicated. *I knew it. Jack's responsible for all the mistletoe around! Or they're in it together.* But I keep that thought to myself. "It's okay, a whole lot of people now have food and fuel in time for Christmas and the storm. That's more important than anything else."

"Pass on my apology to your father, will you?" The old man's tone is so gentle. I nod...and feel my chin trembling.

It's been a long day. I'm kind of emotional, especially after coming down here like this, making myself vulnerable to rejection...and walking right into drama that I never expected. Clearly Aaron, who stands stiffly at his post by the door, didn't expect it either.

"Are you all right?" Whitman asks. "You seem rather sad for someone who was just talking about a stroke of luck."

I press my lips together and look down. This old man is our own version of Grandpa Woodstock, another New York legend. Everyone confides in him. But this is something I can't even bring up to my own father. Not comfortably, anyway.

"I need to ask you something before I get into anything like that," I hedge, needing time. "Are you responsible for the mistletoe all over town?"

I can't help but ask. I saw tons of it on the way up—one more over-the-top element of Christmas in Phoenicia—which only makes me suspect the Whitmans even more. There's bushels of the stuff strung up on the eaves of houses, on the awnings of businesses, in doorways...everywhere.

His eyes twinkle as he accepts the change of subject. "Do you like it?"

"It got me my first kiss with the guy I like, so yes. But I was wondering the reason why you and Jack put that stuff up all over." His smile widens and I hesitate. "You...did...put all those plants up, right?"

"I never said that," he replies cagily. "In fact, I neither set them there with my hands, nor paid for them with my money."

"Did Jack?" *What is going on? Whatever it is, he seems to be way too amused by all of this.*

"I'm afraid that you would have to ask him," is his infuriating answer. "But you aren't actually upset over some handfuls of mistletoe, are you?"

I hesitate. But then I look over at Aaron, who glances my way but stays impassive. Pain grips my heart, and I shake my head.

"Well, the short version is, I've met the guy I want to marry, and he loves me back. And thanks to the mistletoe trick, we kissed earlier. But the guy's older than me, he's got a past, and he doesn't think he deserves me. Neither does my father.

"I was about ready to just start dating the guy and face the consequences later. But now his scumbag brother is in town, trying to make him go away with him forever." My voice gets a little squeaky at the end, and I stop to fight back tears.

"Oh dear. Well, that won't do at all." His brow furrows as he glances out the window at Daniel's silhouette. The man is starting to rub his arms and hunch over.

It's amusing, but it doesn't make me feel much better. "I'm really worried that this creep will blackmail him into leaving. Or do something worse. My friend is strong, but he's the kind of man who will sacrifice everything for someone he cares about. I can't let him leave to protect me. I need to find a way to help him stay."

He looks over at Aaron as well, and then smiles knowingly. "Have you told this man how you feel about him?"

"I...kissed him." I look at him in confusion.

He chuckles. "Oh, I understand. Well, kisses can mean many things, even between lovers. You need to tell him everything. Give him the reasons why you offer your heart. Give him a reason to stay so that he will never give up."

I don't know if he's incredibly wise or drunk as hell and determined to sound profound—the whole town knows he has a weakness for schnapps, especially around the holidays. It works, though. I know what I have to do suddenly, as if a puzzle piece has finally snapped into place. "Thank you," I say quietly. "That won't be easy to do, but I'll...find a way." *If I can.*

"You're quite welcome. Now as I understand it, you probably want a ride out of here so you can avoid that nasty little fellow on the sidewalk." He winks, and I manage a smile.

"Thank you. Yes, I would." Daniel can kiss my ass. I am going to stay out of his way and work as hard as I can against his purposes, by taking Whitman's advice.

I try to sleep for a while after I get home. I manage a nap, still half in my clothes, the covers pulled up to my chin. Around midnight, my father stumbles past my door on the way to the bathroom and peers in, as if confused by the open door. I pretend to be asleep, and he moves on.

Later, I roll over and look at my phone. It's three-thirty in the morning, half an hour to last call. Dad won't be out of bed until it's time to clean up for late morning service.

I shouldn't do this. But Whitman's words ring in my ears. The terrible sense that time is running out, and that I have to act now to make sure that Aaron stays, haunts me as I pull my coat, scarf and gloves back on and stomp into my boots.

I don't quite beat Aaron home. Fresh snow is scraped off on the steps leading up to his door, and his lights are on. I walk up to the door, steeling myself, and knock twice.

I hear excited barking, and then footsteps. A few moments later the door opens, spilling warm air out onto my chilled face, stinging my skin. Aaron barely has his coat off and his hair is still mussed from his hat. His eyes widen when he sees me.

"You shouldn't be here," he protests, and I just smile and brush past him into the trailer. Moose ambles up, thumping his tail. I give him a friendly scratch as Aaron sighs and closes the door. "Dammit, Jules."

"I think I should be here," I insist softly. "I think we have some unfinished business."

"We can't. I can't." He moves past me, settling onto the tiny brown built-in couch and dropping his shaggy head into his hands. "I'm flattered as hell, but—" he starts.

I scowl. "Don't give me that. You want this as badly as I do."

I know that I can put an end to this argument right away, in a way he's not going to have much power to resist. Mostly because he won't want to. But as I move closer to him and I see the bleak look in his eyes, I can't help but hesitate. I want him on board without any kind of...influence.

"Look," I say softly as I stand over him. "I've had a crush on you since I first saw you, okay? Then you became my friend, but I never stopped wanting you. It's only gotten worse over time."

He closes his eyes and tips his head back like I just slapped him. I wonder how he's spent so long alone. How could any woman see that look and not want to hug him and make it better? Because he's big and scary-looking?

So is Moose, and he spends a quarter of his time being cuddled by small children.

"It's been that way for me too," he admits, and my heart aches at the desperation in the back of his eyes. "I don't want anyone else, ever. I want you. No lie. But I'm not good for you. You deserve—"

"I deserve to make my own damn decisions about who I choose to be with," I reply insistently. "I want to be with you. I want you to stay here, and build your life here like you've been doing—but I want you to build it with me. You know we'd be great together—we always are."

He stares at me in amazement.

"Please," I say softly as I walk right up to him, reaching over to run my hands through his shaggy hair. "Don't let anyone get in the way. Not Daniel, not my father. We both want this, don't we?"

I want it—breathlessly. Even if it ends up hurting. I want his body against mine. I want to know what his cock will feel like inside of me. I want to hear him groan with pleasure again, and have him do things to me that will make me scream.

He's in so much pain, and he's so isolated. I want to fix it. "I don't know much about relationships, but when you really want to sleep with the guy who makes you happier than anyone else, isn't that a good thing? Especially if you're both single and into the idea?"

That gets me a thin smile. "Normally, yes. But you're forgetting that you're the preacher's daughter, that you're in training to replace him, and that in general, you're a fucking angel, while I'm..."

"You're what, Aaron?" I glare at him. "If you say you're just like Daniel, you're going to catch hell for it."

He holds up his hands, shaking his head. "No, but I'm not great. Even though I didn't touch that guy they popped me for, I've broken the law a lot. I'm not innocent of wrongdoing.

"I was the club's lookout. I helped guard their clubhouse. I didn't go to that bank knowing Daniel planned to rob it, but I was still there. And I stood there too long yelling at my brother to stop instead of stopping him."

The guilt in his voice tells me that's the real reason he's still so ashamed—maybe even the reason he accepted the jail sentence. He didn't save an innocent man from his brother's fists. He was a bystander instead of a hero. "And you think that I deserve someone who would jump in to protect me right away. No hesitation."

He nods slowly. "Yeah. Yeah, I do."

"It's funny, because you're one of two people in my life that I trust completely to do just that. Otherwise, I would never have fallen in love with you."

He flinches away from my smile like he's staring at the sun, and I wait patiently until he looks back before going on. "That big, bad part of you that you think would scare me off, it only comes out when you need it. I don't know how you were when you were twenty-four, but I know that that part of you would jump to protect me or any other innocent person around here now."

He can't speak right now or look at me, so I bend over and hug him tight, because I can't hold back any more. He wraps his arms around my waist and pulls me against him, burying his face against my breasts.

The feel of his breath against my skin, even through the weave of the scarf, makes me tingle. I tremble slightly, knowing he is about to discover a secret I've carried most of the night, just for him. If anything can pull him from his grief and doubt, it's that.

"Maybe I am a better man now than I was then," he mumbles. "But I still don't deserve you, baby."

"If you want me, you should leave that decision up to me," I murmur soothingly, stroking his hair. "It's my choice. It's yours, too. Respect that."

And then I let out a little laugh, and finally unleash my confession. "Besides, I'm not perfect. I did kind of come here to screw your brains out."

He blinks up at me slowly, astonishment gradually replacing all signs of self-loathing. "Well...damn."

I lean down and kiss him, and he squeezes me tightly against him before his mouth runs down from mine, sliding over my throat. My eyes roll closed. *Oh yes.*

Then his mouth moves lower, and he unties the scarf and throws it aside to get at more of my skin—and stops dead. He notices, finally, that there is no collar to unbutton. The skin beneath is bare.

CHAPTER SEVEN

Julia

"Holy shit," Aaron mumbles, as I slowly tease open the coat to reveal a strip of naked skin that runs down to my navel. It took all my nerve and willpower to walk out my door like this, and the look on his face is worth it.

I'm still blushing, and hoping he's too captivated by the view to notice.

"You...were...really committed to this idea," he murmurs in a tone of delighted shock.

I have to press my lips together to keep from giggling. Deep breath. "Um. Well, yeah.

"I barely know anything about this sort of thing, but I thought I could get your attention by being a little...creative." Because otherwise, what would a man with so much more sexual experience than me want with a boring virgin who knows nothing?

He looks up at my face—and chuckles warmly, shaking his head. "You're blushing like crazy, baby."

"Yeah, well," I say a little more seriously, "if I have to go out of my comfort zone to catch your attention, it's worth it."

He swallows. "You've got all my attention. Always have."

I nod, feeling some of my embarrassment fade. "Good, because if it'd been five degrees colder then I would have frozen my tits off."

"Oh God, no, none of that. I don't want anything bad happening to your tits or any other part of you." He punctuates his words with fervent kisses between the two parts we'd just been discussing, for emphasis.

My knees get wobbly at once. *Oh boy.*

It must have taken a lot of strength for him to pull back from what I hope will become his favorite pillows. But he looks up at me again, and says, "Wait...are you using sex to convince me to stay here? Kind of sinful, isn't it?" Half amused, half dubious.

"I'm here because I love you, and you make me weak in the knees, you big dope." I bend forward to kiss his forehead and he groans as my cleavage ends up in his face. "I really want more than sex out of this, and I think you do too."

"I do," he mumbles. "I'm crazy for you. I'll blow my savings on a ring tomorrow if you want."

"Don't you dare! I don't want anything that fancy." My heart is absolutely singing, and from the way he's practically vibrating out of his clothes, I suspect it's the same for him.

I do pause a moment, though. "Wait. Are you just saying that because my boobs are in your face?"

"Not just," he says dreamily, his voice rather muffled.

"Okay, just checking."

Then he gets back to kissing me there, and his hands slide the coat all the way off of my shoulders, dropping it to the floor. I gasp, and he holds me steady as my knees wobble. I wrap my arms around his shoulders and focus on staying upright while he runs his mouth all over my bare skin.

His breath is warm, his unshaven chin a little scratchy, and his lips softer than I expected. Now and again, the hot dart of his tongue seeks me out as he holds me—at all my pulse points, the hollow of my throat, every bit of my breasts, before finally focusing on the edges of one and circling inward. I start to pant and whimper through my closed lips.

His mouth closes over my nipple, and I let out a sharp cry. My hands cling to his shoulders as he pushes forward, sucking in long strokes. The sensation leaves me drugged in moments—I'm tingling all over, moaning in time with his pulls as my vulva starts to ache with need.

It feels incredible...better than any of my imaginings. Somehow, it starts to feel even better every second, as I become more turned on than I have ever been in my life. My cries of pleasure fill the small space shamelessly, and I can tell it turns him on—he shudders every time I moan, and he eventually responds to each one with a low grunt of pleasure.

He changes nipples every once in a while, teasing me into a frenzy. Eventually my legs start shaking, and the thermals I'm wearing on my lower body feel like they're smothering me. I croon wordlessly, not able to form words while his mouth remains on me.

He holds me firmly, and I sway and cling to him and make noises. I've lost the ability to do much more. My heart pounds in my ears, and every shift of his lips against my nipple sends fresh electric jolts of bliss through me.

If I had known it would be this good, I would have chased him down topless well before now, I manage to think. He sucks harder, nibbling and licking in between long pulls, and suddenly I can't even think. I rock against him, my whole mind overwhelmed by sensation.

I manage to step out of my boots and kick them away, glad to be rid of them—wishing I could be rid of everything. I want his hands all over me. But when I let go of him to try to shuck my thermals off, my legs almost give out.

He grabs me by the hips...and then runs his hands down over the globes of my ass, caressing and kneading them through the fabric before pushing the thermals off and doing the same to my bare skin. The cool air blows against my dripping, aching sex, but does nothing to lessen the heat there.

His rough hand slides smoothly around to cup my vulva while the other grips my ass to steady me, and his fingers tease against the insides of my thighs. No one has ever touched me there, and for a moment, even though it's him, and I'm practically in ecstasy already, I almost freeze up.

It's too much. But I breathe deep and whimper my way through it as he starts to rub and knead my whole mound at once. He does it gently and softly at first, then more roughly, dipping his fingers in between my lower lips and stroking them up and down.

My eyes roll in their sockets uncontrollably as powerful jolts of pleasure run through me with every stroke of his fingers. He finds a rhythm quickly, and though his touch is delicate, he will not let me go.

I unsnap his vest impatiently and start unbuttoning his shirt. My hands shake; I fumble clumsily, sometimes having to stop just to hang onto him. Finally he stops caressing and suckling me, leaving me standing there trembling and staring down at him in shock.

He smiles lazily, his eyes burning, and shrugs out of his vest and shirt, then strips off his thermal underneath and tosses them both aside. I look down at him, his barrel chest and burly arms tattooed with bluish ink, and the thin, curving scar that runs along his side. I have to squash the sudden impulse to lean down and kiss it better.

Then I catch sight of him unbuckling his belt, and suddenly that has all my attention.

His belly flexes as he sits forward and shucks the leather jeans and thermals off with one firm shove. His cock springs up against his scarred belly and I stare at it for a moment, a little shocked. *I guess every part of him is huge,* I think through a haze of lust.

"I won't hurt you, baby," he promises, coaxing me forward onto his broad thighs. I clamber onto him, sitting high, not sure what to do next. His cock brushes against my belly, and I feel that ache deep in my vulva again.

He starts to caress me between my legs, and this time he slowly dips the tip of his finger into me, getting it slick with my juices as he watches my face for my response. I whimper, gasp and squirm, wanting more, and let out a little moan of disappointment when he draws his finger out again.

He starts stroking my clit again in that same way, softly, but without ever letting up, and my back arches as I push my hips forward. He moves slightly, and as I lift up on my knees with my legs on the couch on either side of him, I feel the head of his cock pushing at my opening.

For just a moment, I don't know if I can handle this, and I hesitate. But then I smile to myself. *Of course I can.* It's new...but I'm driving, and the sight of him shaking and panting under me as I roll my hips to start taking him in makes me bold.

"Unh!" He shudders as I sink down on him, head lolling, and I feel a rush of power as I bear down. It hurts...but only for a moment as my unaccustomed body takes him in. Then the pressure on my walls, feeling him stretching me, rubbing against sensitive spots inside me, starts intensifying the pleasure of his caresses.

I straddle him, arms around him, and kiss him. He groans into my mouth as I rock my hips experimentally. His eyes are glazed. I can do anything I want to him right now, and he'll probably beg for more.

We move together while he continues to stimulate me, his hand tireless between my thighs while I moan and roll my hips unconsciously around him. "Oh that's so good, baby," he purrs in my ear. "Harder?"

"Yes," I whimper, and he starts lifting his hips against me more roughly, grunting softly with the effort. His hand moves steadily in time with his thrusts, and he bears down just a little more, leaving me gasping with pleasure and grinding against his hand.

He pushes his cock into me again and again; the pain dissolves, and my muscles start to tighten around him as my whole body tingles with pleasure. I can hear myself moaning and crying out for more, and he pants through his teeth before leaning me back so he can fasten his mouth onto one of my nipples again.

The triple sensation leaves me sobbing uncontrollably with joy. Something's coming. Each stroke of his finger, suck of his mouth, and thrust of his cock feels better, and better, and *better*...

He stops.

I cry out in protest and squirm against him, but he just smiles and grabs me by the hips before lifting me and standing up. Still inside of me, he kisses me, and then starts walking us slowly toward his bed. We kiss the whole way.

He starts panting again partway there, and pushes me against the wall, bracing me against it while he thrusts in roughly. His surging cock stokes the flame again. I hang on for dear life, stunned by how primal it is, and my breathing fragments into tiny, desperate sips of air.

I feel my body tensing deliciously...and then he stops again.

"You're torturing me," I moan. I can't stand it.

I don't know what it feels like to cum. I'm a little scared of the power of all these feelings. I just know that if I don't relieve the sweet, agonizing tension in my body soon, I'm going to start crying.

Finally, we reach the bed. He settles on the edge then leans me back again, and starts rolling his hips under me as he starts stimulating me once more. "Don't stop this time," I whimper. "Please...please..."

"Of course, baby." His voice is hoarse and full of tenderness, even as he fucks my brains out.

He thrusts and strokes, his mouth at the pulse in my throat, our bodies straining against each other as that wonderful tension builds up in me again. I'm gasping for air. Little cries and whimpers explode from me and grow into a strained crescendo as the pleasure swells between my thighs.

I'm almost there—

And then it comes—and I lose my mind for long, exquisite moments.

I throw my head back and let out a long wail of pleasure as ecstasy rips through me in waves. I grind against his cock, feeling my muscles clench around it, intensifying the pleasure and satisfying the hungry ache inside of me.

Still feverish, I look down; he's fallen back, eyes closed, lips parted, his hips lifting under me with desperation now. I smile dizzily and start to ride him despite my sudden exhaustion, circling and bucking my hips.

"Oh! Oh baby—!" he shouts, and then grabs my hips and starts thrusting upward into me hard while I ride him with everything I have left.

I watch his face, heart full of love and desire, as his eyes widen and then squeeze closed. His lips part—and then he starts to shout.

They're just little bursts of sound at first, coming every time his cock sinks into me. But then they grow louder, longer, hoarser, even as my body starts to clench around him again. I groan through my teeth and watch him as he tenses, and his hips practically lift me off the bed.

Then his voice rises in a roar, and he thrusts deep a last time, his cock twitching and spilling heat inside of me.

He collapses back onto the bed gasping for air, as I wobble over him, my muscles going slack. He catches me and pulls me into his arms. I lie on his heaving chest...and feel every problem in the world drift wonderfully away.

CHAPTER EIGHT

Aaron

I watch Julia sleep, my whole body still shaking. I haven't ever busted so hard in my life. I think I started screaming.

That's all right. The trailer's well insulated, and there's no one around for a half acre on either side. And as I lie there, feeling so light and loose that I could float off the mattress, I think to myself: *I could go for another round of that.*

Every night, for the rest of my life. It's more a taste of Heaven than a man like me deserves, but she's offering, and I'm starved for it.

I still don't feel like I'm good enough for her. I'm not sure that any mortal man could be—but then again, I'm biased. And since she keeps insisting on pushing the issue, I figure I had better just find a way to be an even better man.

I brush stray hairs off her forehead as I stare down at her. *I knocked her out. Poor baby.*

I didn't even mean to. But that look of astonishment she wore before her eyes rolled closed told me volumes about her inexperience. I'm humbled that she chose me to be her first.

Damn, I'm glad I held out so long. But seriously, this is the first time that my brother's nickname for me doesn't seem ironic.

I doze for just a little while, bundled with her in my comforters, before her warm, curving softness and the scent of sex wakes me. I'm not surprised that I have a raging boner.

It's still dark. I should be waking her up and telling her to dress and sneak back home before her father wakes up.

I start kissing her neck instead.

She murmurs in her sleep and rolls toward me, one arm sliding limply over my back. My cock aches fiercely, but I take my time, kissing and caressing her awake. She's so warm and relaxed now, and when I slide my hand under her and start stroking her ass, she croons low in her throat and opens her eyes.

"Hi, baby," I purr in her ear. I can barely see her smile in the dimness. When we kiss, she responds at once, sliding a hand down my body and settling it on my cock.

I let out a surprised grunt, and she smiles against my mouth as she starts to explore my shaft with her fingers. Her touch is electric, yet delicate, mapping every inch of my erection until I'm panting. I gently pull her hand away.

"Make love to me," she murmurs, rolling onto her back and running her nails over my hips. "I want you inside me again, now."

Wow. I climb onto her and settle over her gently, working my cock into her as slowly as I can force myself. She gasps and shimmies her hips, lifting herself impatiently to take more of me in.

Her silken folds close around me, and my back arches, head thrown back as I fight the urge to cum right away. "Oh—oh!" I shout with pleasure, and she wraps her arms and legs around me welcomingly.

We move together, and for a few long, luxuriant thrusts I

can't focus on anything but the feel of her hot, slick flesh against mine. Then I remember myself, and start caressing her again.

Her back arches as I lift up a little and slip a hand between us, gently pinching her cunt lips together around her clit and stroking and kneading her. She starts gasping and squirms even more. I thrust in deep and stay there, letting her writhe around my cock as her muscles gradually go tighter and tighter around me.

"Come on, baby," I encourage her as she starts to tremble and pant under me. Her eyes roll closed, and her mouth opens in a long gasp. "Come on, let go. You're almost there."

My hips start moving reflexively as she grinds against me. I start to pant as well, and struggle to keep my hand moving and my body from cutting loose before she does. The glow between us is so intense that it threatens to burn up my stamina.

Her nails dig into my back as all her muscles tighten and she presses herself hard up against me. Her gasps turn into that musical, rising cry again, broken up by her panting, as she grinds against me with all her strength. I feel my own body ramp up toward climax—and then her contractions drag me that last inch as her pussy massages my shaft irresistibly.

I pound into her roughly, growling with bliss as she squirms under me and squeals with delight. Now and again, her muscles ripple over me again; I shout hoarsely at the extra jolt of pleasure, my voice rising with hers.

I fight to stay on the edge as long as I can—and then go rocketing over it, roaring with joy as I shoot my load into her again. "Yes—!"

This time, I am the one who almost faints.

I barely manage to catch myself as my body goes limp, and I roll off of her, gathering her into my arms. She whimpers softly, eyelids weighed down from exhaustion. "There you go," I purr in her ear. "There you go, baby. I love you."

I tuck my comforters around us again and drift off with her. The last thing I sense as I fall asleep is Moose hopping up to lie contentedly across the foot of the bed.

I'm so loopy from sex and satisfaction that it takes me a few moments to jump out of bed when Moose starts barking. It's got to be some time later; there's faint light coming in from outside.

I can hear the anger in my dog's bark as I yank on my clothes and grab my bow. Then I hear the thumps as of someone trying to bust in my garage door, and I know.

Fucking Daniel.

I come walking out with Moose on a leash in case my brother has a gun. Daniel is there, trying to get in my shed door with a crowbar. He's getting nowhere against the heavy-duty lock. *Idiot.*

He sees me—and then sees Moose, and his eyes get very wide again. Once again the guy's been drinking, and it's fucking with his judgment. "The fuck are you doing, Daniel?" I demand.

It's not even dawn yet. Well below freezing. My spit crackles as it hits the grass and I walk in his direction quickly, the crossbow I'm not supposed to have pointed at him with my free hand.

He drops the crowbar and steps back. "I told you I'd make trouble for you until you agreed to come with me," he stammers, his eyes glued to Moose, who has stopped barking and is now just growling.

"And I told you that was a stupid fucking idea, Daniel. I've got you on my security cameras breaking and entering." I point up at the deer cams I have hidden in the pines on either side of the shed entrance.

"You'd set the pigs on me? They'll put me away for life!" Moose's growling drops an octave and jumps several decibels in response to Daniel raising his voice, and my brother presses back against the shed door.

"Now you listen here, you little shit. Back when I was an idealistic kid whose life you wrecked, I thought I owed you because we were family. But then I went in the hole for ten years and served four years parole for a crime I was trying to stop your ass from committing."

He holds his hands over his head, eyes huge now, as if suddenly realizing that he's put himself into deep, deep shit, and there's very little he can do about it but beg. "Hey, now, come on. I'm desperate here. I need your fucking help! Don't you get it?"

"Oh, I get it. You've screwed up in yet another state, and you want me around to keep you safe from however many hoods down in New Orleans want to kick your sorry ass. But as I was saying, I've already gone above and beyond for your dumpster-fire ass, and that was the last time."

I advance on him, short-leashing Moose so he can't take a chomp out of my brother before I have my say. "If I had gone down for something I'd actually done, that would be one thing. But even all of that was shit you dragged me into.

"I owe you nothing. In fact, you owe me. And the credit store is closed, brother mine. Fuck off."

He swallows, taking a deep, shuddery breath. "You know, I know you have me on camera trying to get at your bike, but uh...you're also on camera with a crossbow, and you've got a felony record just like me now." His eyes glitter.

I stare at him coldly, unable to believe that this dumb son of a bitch is still pushing me. "Okay, fine, we're at a Mexican standoff over that. You still can't really mess with me. You've got nothing on me that can force me to leave."

The door to the trailer clicks open, and Julia walks out sleepily. Her hair is mussed, her eyes are drowsy, and she has a love bite showing where her scarf is askew.

My eyes widen slightly. *Shit.*

Daniel looks between her and me, and a slow grin breaks

across his face. "Yeah, I do. I've been asking around, brother mine. Isn't that the preacher's twenty-year-old virgin daughter?"

"Twenty-one," I say defensively, as she sees us and freezes.

"And not a virgin any more, I'll bet," he laughs, and my heart sinks.

CHAPTER NINE

Julia

"What do we do?" I can't quite keep the panic out of my voice. I've just made it that much easier for Daniel to uproot Aaron from here. All Daniel has to do is tell my father, and even if Dad doesn't drive Aaron out of town, he'll probably make Aaron so uncomfortable that he'll flee on his own.

I'm finding out the hard way that nothing kills a good afterglow like being caught by the wrong person. But I'll be damned if I let some drunk, corrupt bastard mess up my future with Aaron.

"Well, either I find my brother and kick his ass before he can talk to your dad, and maybe I'll go to jail for it. Or I let him spill the beans to your dad, and I probably get run out of town." He sounds so frustrated that I feel like a complete idiot. I got him into this.

We're cuddled together for a few stolen moments on his couch before I have to hurry home and grab a nap before Dad gets up. "Let me help. I can reason with my father."

He shakes his head. "How the hell are you planning to do that?"

"I'll find a way, okay? Besides, it's better that he hears about our relationship from me than from some horrible asshole who is just saying stuff to drive us apart." My voice shakes as I plead with him.

He frowns and folds his arms. "I certainly think we had better warn your father and some others about Daniel being in town. Not the deputy, though. Earl will just think I invited Daniel here, and that things went south."

"Darnit. Earl." I sigh. I'm getting sick of prejudiced people, even if they generally mean well. "One day, I'll get every last one of them to stop judging people they barely know."

"Honey, you're not gonna be able to work miracles," he says sadly, but I shake my head.

"I believe people around here can be better, or I wouldn't want to take over my dad's job." I look him firmly in the eye. "Meanwhile, I'll go home and warn Dad about Daniel. If we're lucky, maybe people will be madder at him for stirring things up during the holidays than they will be at you for having a shitty brother."

I kiss him goodbye, aware of his taste in my mouth, his scent all over me. The little sore spots where he's marked me and the melting warmth deep in my belly are souvenirs from our lovemaking. I feel like I'm carrying him with me, and it gives me strength on the dark, cold walk home.

Strange things are happening in this town, and I have no idea how to take some of it. I don't mind pranks, windfalls of food, even the odd blizzard. But a drunken older brother who is scheming to take away my man? I can't wait to see the back of that bastard Daniel.

I'm worried I won't notice him if he's following me on the walk back, and I take a circuitous route just to make sure there's no one behind me. I'm walking back down the hill toward our church when I hear a scuffle up ahead.

I carefully move up to the corner and peek around it—and see Daniel getting his butt kicked. Not by Aaron, though. The woman in question is a tall, statuesque redhead, way underdressed for the cold, and currently beating Daniel over the head with her Fendi bag while screaming at him at the top of her lungs. Lights are already going on in the houses nearby.

"What the fuck, bitch! Just give me your purse and stop making problems!"

"Take it, then!" She thwacks him with it so hard that it sounds like she's got a brick stowed in her little purse. Then she yanks out an honest-to-God canister of bear mace and blasts him with it.

I just stand there staring. *Oh my God. Who is this crazy city woman and where did You find her just in time for this guy to get a much-needed stiletto heel up his butt?*

Daniel goes down yelling and holding his face. The redhead starts stalking off. I'm still hesitating about stepping in when Earl, out cruising the town for lost drunks, bleeps his cruiser siren and pulls up to the biker.

I draw back behind the corner, blinking slowly. Then I call up Aaron. "Hey, sweetie? Before you go back to sleep, uh...I think we won't have to worry about your brother for a few days..."

I leave him laughing as I walk the rest of the way home.

The reprieve is more than welcome. It means Christmas without interruption. It means that if we're very lucky, Earl and the guys at the state police will check warrants in New York and New Orleans, and that will be the last we see of Daniel.

It really looks like Aaron's luck has changed. And I know that mine sure has.

Dad is still passed out in his room when I get home. I'm slack from exhaustion and sexual satisfaction, and I have to wrestle with a faint sense of guilt as I walk past his door. But as I change into my flannels, most of what I feel is contentment.

We'll find a way to work this out. God willing, we'll even find a way to get Dad on board.

I don't shower. I go to bed with the scent of Aaron on my body, and fall asleep smiling.

The next two days are a busy, happy blur. Holiday festivities mix with storm preparation, and by the time our small Christmas dinner comes around, both my father and I are ready for a reprieve.

Unfortunately, the break we get is thanks to a big Christmas snowstorm.

"Are all the storm windows in place?" my father frets a little. "Is the snow removal gear inside? It won't do us any good if it's out in the shed."

"It's fine, Dad, I handled it all." Compared to my dad, I'm so calm that I could be floating on a cloud right now. I snuck out to Aaron's trailer early this morning again, and we made love until we both couldn't move.

I would be doing that again tonight, but the damn storm's coming in—two to three feet of snow expected in twenty-four hours. At least it gives me an excuse to sleep in tomorrow.

I come to stand with my dad and look out the window at the big flakes starting to swirl past outside. The sky is leaden, the wind keeps rising to a whine in the eaves, and my father tenses up each time the windows rattle.

"So, this brother of Aaron's made bail?" He's trying to make conversation, but I can tell from the topic that he's looking for reassurance.

"Yes, he did, down in Kingston. I know it wasn't Aaron who paid it." I wish he was here. I would just feel safer with my man around now that his brother is loose, even if he's an hour's drive away in a growing blizzard.

"Are you sure?" he eyes me worriedly.

"Pretty sure. No one's madder about that creep being out than Aaron. He doesn't want Daniel anywhere near here."

"Well, he'll probably get his wish, at least for the night. Only a crazy person would be out driving in this." My father rubs his face. "What did they say the chances are of a blackout?"

"We have three generators now, and Aaron's bringing by two more in a little while. I just got off the phone with him. If people end up blacked out at length, we can have heat, light, phone-charging stations, and food for them for three days." I touch my father's arm.

He's starting to answer when someone knocks hard on the front door. "That must be him now!" I cry out excitedly and run down the stairs.

It's a stupid mistake. The kind that makes you wish you could rewind the world by thirty seconds and make a different choice. I'm inexperienced, in love, and have underestimated the determination of a crazy person with a vendetta. None of those things are really an excuse.

I throw the door open before checking through the peephole, and before I can do anything, Daniel is shoving his way inside.

CHAPTER TEN

Aaron

I'm doing the most exhilarating mental calculations in the world as I stick both generators in my sidecar. *If all she wants is an inexpensive ring, I can go down to the city and buy a nice one as soon as we're through with this storm. I can do that on this next paycheck without dipping into savings much.*

Moose looks at me and whines. "Sorry, big guy, no room for you and the cargo."

Once he's seen to and shut up in my trailer with the heat running, I take the bike down to the church. I'm determined to make sure that whatever happens with this storm, Julia and her dad will have power, heat, and light to spare no matter how many people shelter there.

As I drive, I'm going over my speech. "Reverend, I have to come clean with you. Your daughter and I are crazy about each other, and I want to marry her."

Simple, straightforward. It's probably best. Especially since, if I ask for his blessing now, it won't matter anymore what Daniel says.

I'm starting to feel almost optimistic about my talk with the Reverend when I see a car parked almost sideways in the church driveway. It's a brown sedan, battered, one tire flat, and the side window cracked. I stare at it, knowing a stolen and drunkenly parked car when I see one.

Daniel, you son of a bitch!

I park my bike and break into a run through the snow, thinking fast. I know the grounds; I know the building; I know that the storm doors on the house's basement coal chute need to be replaced and will be unlocked.

I run around the side of the church toward the house, headed straight for that rust-colored, slanted door. I pull it open as quietly as I can, and scramble down the steps beyond. The basement is black, but I always have a light on my belt.

I don't have any weapons, I think as I sneak up the basement steps and listen at the door. I can hear faint voices. Probably coming from the living room, by the sound of them. I quickly push the door open and sneak into the kitchen.

For a moment, I am tempted. The knife block on the counter is within arm's reach. I could grab the biggest knife or the cleaver. I could end this in a very final way...

I could kill my brother in front of the love of my life and her pastor father, who is already nervous around me. *Absolutely not. I'll find another way.*

As I make my way down the hall, I hear the conversation going on and my heart sinks.

"This isn't a family meeting," Julia insists. "This is a hostage situation. You're not wanted here. The only reason we have to sit here is because if we don't, you're gonna beat the hell out of both of us. You said it yourself."

"That's right," Daniel laughs. "I did. See, Reverend, my poor, stupid brother is gonna leave with me tonight, and we're going down to New Orleans where the fucking Snow Queen isn't on a cocaine binge and working overtime. If he doesn't, I'll make his life a living Hell. Starting with rearranging his little slut girlfriend's face."

"How dare you talk about my daughter this way!" The Reverend sounds ready to fall over in fear, but he's still standing up for Julia. I admit I'm a little proud of him.

Outside, the wind is starting to really howl. It worries me, but nowhere near as much as the idea of my brother and Julia in the same room together.

I do a quick check around the door frame and see Daniel sitting with his back to me, idly holding Julia by the hair. His coat is off, in a pile on the floor. He doesn't have a gun.

He does have his hands on my sweetheart, though.

"You tell your daddy what you've been doing, you little whore. Don't make a liar out of me, or I'm gonna start knocking your teeth out."

"Let go of me, you creep! Dad already knows I'm in love with Aaron—"

Daniel lets out a laugh as her sharp cry of shock—or maybe pain—cuts off her words. "But does he know you're sneaking around behind his back *fucking* Aaron?"

Oh fuck, I think, wincing.

Everyone's voice erupts at once; exclamations, arguing, total chaos. I see my chance, and bolt into the room.

Julia turns and sees me coming. Her face lights up, and she immediately elbows Daniel in the side and pulls away from him when his grip loosens. I crash into him from behind a second later.

Daniel yells in shock as I lift him entirely off his feet, "What the fuck!?"

"Sorry I'm late," I tell the Reverend and Julia as my brother kicks and wiggles in my grip. "I was having trouble fitting both the generators in my sidecar."

"How the Hell did you get inside the house?" Daniel is still struggling like a kid, but he's getting nowhere.

"I've worked on the place for years," I reply coolly. I look over at the Reverend. "I'm also sorry for any trouble this jackass has caused. He's on his way out the door."

The Reverend gets over his shock quickly and heaves a sigh of relief. "Yes, please get him out of my house."

"Wait, wait, wait! Come on, now! Do you really want to take this guy's side? He's a felon! We're in the same club!" Daniel probably weighs a ton as he twists around, struggling, but I'm so angry I can't feel it. Instead, I'm fighting the urge to break his damn back.

"We *were* in the same club," I growl. "I gave up my freedom to save yours, and now I'm done with you and that life."

"Oh shut the fuck up, you stupid bastard. You chose to be a damn martyr. You chose to take the fall in my place. Yeah, I told you to do it, and I promised to take care of you while you were inside and to leave you alone once you were free. But you were the one who was dumb enough to believe me!"

His taunts hit home, hard. My muscles start to tighten around his ribs. I can literally break him over my knee if I want.

Julia and her father are watching me. I stop tightening my grip.

"So it's true," the Reverend muses. "He accepted incarceration so that you would remain free, when he did nothing to that man."

"I told you—" Julia sighs and goes quiet, shaking her head.

"Look," Daniel waves his hands, still looking ridiculous dangling from my grip. "We're both criminals. We belong together, well away from decent people like you and your...lovely daughter. If you're gonna throw me out, throw him out as well!"

My heart sinks. I sigh, and look at the Reverend. "I'll leave if you want."

He scowls at me, surprising me. "Don't you dare. We have a lot to talk about. As for him...I'm calling Earl to come pick him up." He walks over to the coffee table and picks up his phone. His hands are shaky, but he seems all right.

I nod and cart Daniel over to the door. "You can wait outside," I tell him, doing my job even though it's my night off.

"But wait, my jacket," he protests as Julia gets up to unlock the door and open it for me. "Come on, man, I'll freeze."

"Earl will be up in five to ten minutes. This town is tiny," I reply patiently as I step out onto the porch.

"It's ten degrees out—" he yells in a final protest.

"Exactly." I pitch him off the porch and into a snowbank. He lands safely but sinks deep enough that he's stuck flailing like a turtle on its back.

I go back inside and shut the door on him. Good riddance to that relic of my past—now, to face my future.

I square my shoulders and walk back in to face the Reverend. Everything I rehearsed has fled my mind, but I still manage to look him in the eyes. "I'll explain everything," I start, but he shakes his head.

"I don't want to hear it," he replies in a low, tired voice. "I know I misjudged you in many ways. But whether Daniel's accusation about you and my daughter is true or not, we're not talking about that. I already have a headache."

Julia sits quietly in a chair nearby, looking both nervous and determined.

"What should we talk about then, Reverend?"

"We're going to talk about the fact that you are not laying another hand on my daughter unless you lead with a ring. That is one thing I will never compromise on, and if Julia weren't so wildly in love, she'd likely agree."

Julia speaks up. "Actually, I do agree."

The Reverend blinks at her. "Oh." Then he looks between

the two of us. "And you? Are you ready to commit to her, and wear a symbol of that commitment?"

Damn. This is all happening fast. Except it isn't. We've been in love for years. We've only just started finally admitting it and doing something about it.

"I guess I'm just surprised that you changed your mind so fast," I admit.

"I haven't changed my mind. Not entirely. But when I discovered that Julia was in love with you, I prayed for a sign. Tonight, I got it." He takes a deep breath.

"You had every reason to run in here and do some violence to your brother that would silence him and vindicate you. He just taunted you more. And while he confirmed that you truly are a better man than he will ever be, he also admitted just how little he valued the biggest sacrifice of your life." The Reverend goes over to the china cabinet and fishes out three snifters and a bottle of brandy.

He pours one for each of us as he goes on. "You did not avenge yourself. You just subdued him and got rid of him."

Outside we can see flashing red and blue lights as Earl picks up my lightly chilled brother. For the first time in a long time, it doesn't make me sick inside to see signs of a cop around. "I can't claim to be a better guy than I was and then not act like one."

"Well, I'm glad you did." He coughs into his fist and starts passing out glasses. "Now, I am going to have a nice brandy, and then go to bed, because I have absolutely had it with this evening. I expect you two to behave while under my roof."

"Yes, Reverend," I chuckle as Julia, wearing a look of deep relief, comes to sit beside me. We clink glasses, and I take a welcome drink.

It's going to be a test of my willpower to stay out of bed with my new love until the storm is over, and I can buy her a ring. But her father is right—it's what she deserves.

The next year is going to be amazing. I can just tell. Even if the rest of the year is full of storms, we'll weather them together.

Her hand slips into mine as her father turns to put the bottle away, and I give it a squeeze. Now I will have two things to thank God for every morning.

I'm looking forward to it.

The End.

SIGN UP TO RECEIVE FREE BOOKS

Sign Up to Receive Free E-Books and Audiobook Codes.

Would you like to read **The Unexpected Nanny, Dirty Little Virgin** and **other romance books** for **free**?

You can sign up to receive these free e-books and audiobooks by typing this link into your browser:

https://www.steamyromance.info/free-books-and-audiobooks-hot-and-steamy/

Or this one:

https://www.steamyromance.info/the-unexpected-nanny-free/

PREVIEW OF A KISS OF WINTER
A SECOND CHANCE CHRISTMAS ROMANCE (DREAMS FULFILLED BOOK 3)

By Scarlett King

Synopsis

Andi Carter and David Delgado are best friends and partners in a ghost hunting organization in Upstate New York. They also used to be married—but they don't like to talk about that. It was a mistake, they were too young…and there were some issues in their sex life. Once again—they don't talk about it. Of course, now they're back in the land of unresolved sexual tension, Mulder and Scullying their way through cases—except that he's the skeptic.

They hear about a bizarre case in picturesque Phoenicia, and head out to a bed and breakfast to investigate for themselves. Once there, the romantic setting creates hilarious levels of awkwardness as their memory of their comically terrible first try intrudes on any hope for a second chance. They try to focus on the investigation, but can't seem to sort out where the mistletoe came from or how it manages to keep being replaced.

When a few of the locals start flirting with them, unexpected jealousy and rekindling of desire force the pair to work on solving their own romantic issues. Their rekindled passions end up reminding them of the love they share, and give them a second chance now that they are mature enough to form a committed relationship. In that way their hunt is a success, even if the mistletoe incident remains a mystery forever.

Andi

David and I don't talk about our short-lived marriage. It gets in the way of our friendship and our partnership. We're supposed to be trying to explain the inexplicable—of the paranormal variety, not the romantic—and bickering about our ill-fated romance isn't the way to do it.

We were so young back then, and though he was never able to satisfy me when we were both inexperienced and didn't have a clue, being cooped up with him in this romantic little town has me noticing how much David has changed—and has me wondering just how much he's truly learned in the years since we broke up.

With mistletoe hanging everywhere in this town, there's no doubt that love is in the air. But can that love be ours, or did we already waste our one chance? 'Tis the season for many things, but are we brave enough to let it be the season of second chances?

David

Once upon a time I was a complete idiot—too damn young and inexperienced and cocky to boot. And because of that, I messed up my chances with the woman I've always loved.

Unrequited love is never easy, but it's a whole hell of a lot harder when it includes a successful business and a lifelong friendship. Even years after I blew my chance, I just can't let go of the feeling that Andi is the only one for me.

I never want to see Andi hurt again, so when she comes down with a mysterious winter-related illness, all my protective instincts come creeping in. I've already lost this woman once, and I'll be damned if it happens again.

Now I just need to make her see that we're worth a second chance—and if I need to let a little Christmas magic run its course to make that happen...well then, who am I to say that miracles don't exist?

CHAPTER 1

Andi

"Good morning, sunshine!"

David strolls in through the connecting door between our suites and pulls the curtains aside on all the windows, sending thin winter sunlight trickling into the room. He's got that shit-eating grin on his handsome face that used to annoy me back when we were married.

I lob my pillow at him, eyes bleary, but my aim is still perfect after five years. It bounces off his chest, and he looks down, then snorts and scoops it up. I roll over and bury my face in my remaining pillow. "Go away! It's freezing and before nine."

"Yes, and this is the Catskills. People start their days at dawn here—we're missing chances for interviews. Besides, it was your idea for us to spend our Christmas up here." The slight edge to his voice reminds me of how hard it had been to sell him on this investigation when I first learned of the events transpiring in this town.

Our partnership as paranormal investigators—just like our

friendship—survived our disastrous six-month marriage with little more than some awkwardness and regret. But here I've had to live with him again for over a week and a half, and it's reminding me of why we broke up. "Yes, I know. Just give me...half an hour."

I have also always hated that he's a morning person.

"Nuh-uh. You decided to spend half the night driving over to the county hospital to chase down those frostbite cases, and you straight up told me that you didn't want us knocked off schedule because of it." He comes over and crouches down beside the bed, so his face is level with mine. "So get your cute ass up. We have a mystery to solve."

He was right. And it wasn't just any mystery, either. It was the paranormal event of a lifetime—a genuine Christmas miracle that started almost two weeks ago with thousands of witnesses. It was an event so enormous that even news and social media have noticed and have been rationalizing and celebrating it instead of denying it outright.

Within a week of the first sighting on December 23rd, Phoenicia, New York, had already gained the nickname Mistletoe Village, becoming a destination for romantic-minded snow bunnies from all over the East Coast—and beyond. The bed and breakfasts have filled up, people are renting out spare rooms in their houses for some extra cash, and over a hundred couples have gotten engaged here so far. Tourists, reporters, bloggers, and curiosity seekers are mingling with the local population, filling up the restaurants, cafes, and bars as the early January chill drives them inside.

I can hear the rustle and chatter of the crowd down on the street even through my double-glazed window. *Dammit, he's right.*

I sigh into my bedding and roll over to look at David. He's cute, both in personality and looks, and I really like the guy. But

I also find him really annoying at times, which is part of why the whole marriage thing never worked out.

We're still best friends though, and I wouldn't be able to run Astraea Paranormal without him. He's the tech half to my lore half. While I'm doing interviews, conducting research, and recording EVPs, he's checking for magnetic fields, seeking rational explanations, and making sure that whatever we come up with can't be easily debunked. He also handles the technical and scheduling details, making sure we can get where we need to be and do what we need to do—and do it on time.

And that's why I'm waking up on January the third in a bed and breakfast in the Catskills with my ex-husband in my face.

"Dammit, Dave," I grumble, but I know he's right.

David Delgado, tech genius and occasional jackass who was born with a silver spoon in his mouth, flops into a bedside chair as I drag myself out of bed. He's the classic tall, dark, and handsome type with thick, coffee-colored hair, big brown eyes, and an easy smile. To top it off, I know he's got an amazing body under that turtleneck and jeans—but I don't let myself think about that any more.

When he was younger, he was almost cherubic looking. But he was also a bit of an immature pain in the butt back then, so... it was a trade-off.

And that brings us to Reason Number Two that we should never have married: we were too damn young to know what we were doing—in and out of bed. It would have helped if David had taken instruction better, but I have my own faults, too.

I rub my eyes, blinking several times. "Unh. Okay. My notes from last night's interviews are on the laptop. Take a look at them while I clean up." I push myself out of bed as he gets up to go for my laptop case.

As I walk past him, I hear his breath catch. Still half asleep, I haven't pulled my sleeping shirt down to cover where it's ridden up my thighs in back. I grumble and tug the hem down over my ass, remembering how I used to love turning him on by accident like that.

"Y-yeah. Okay," he replies like a startled kid. I can't help but smile a little. Okay, well, maybe I still like it some.

My marriage to David was the biggest and most regrettable mistake I've made in my life. We were too young—in our early twenties—and though David is sweet and would never hurt me, he was even more in over his head than I was. He was too immature and irritating to live with, and it sometimes felt like I was helping to raise my younger brother all over again.

As I scrub off in the shower with the door open, I hear him clicking away on my laptop. "I'm really starting to think someone is messing with our investigation," I hear him sigh.

"That Jack Whitman guy?" I think about Whitman as I lather up my hair. He's a local—and a world-class skier, snow sculptor, and billionaire playboy with an eccentric father. Mischievous, creative and—I'm starting to suspect—probably the reason why we're here.

He also happens to be ridiculously sexy in that slim, toned, sleek way that is almost androgynous. With his pale white skin, black hair, his father's brilliant blue eyes, and one of those smiles that light up the street, it's a real shame that he's even less mature than David.

"Whitman and whoever else is conspiring with him to do this. There is absolutely no way that mistletoe could just appear hanging just about everywhere in the entire town, with new sprigs somehow popping up every night, without an awful lot of help." I hear more typing.

"You're presuming that nothing paranormal is going on." I have soap in my eyes. "Crap." I bend into the spray to rinse it out and then rinse out my hair, enjoying the hot water on my skin. New York winters leave a chill that's hard to get out of your bones, but a shower or a soak does the trick, even if only for a short while.

"It's my job to presume that nothing paranormal is going on." He taps a few keys. "Did you actually find out anything from the nurses?"

"They wouldn't let me record, but I got some follow-ups. The Marysville Hospital serves this entire area, and until they get an accident or a bad bug going around, they're usually pretty quiet." I turn the water off and stand in the steam, rubbing conditioner into my thick auburn hair.

"So the frostbite thing stood out?"

"Not for that in particular. They get frostbite cases every year, and there was just a big storm. But no. I was pretty much able to verify that it was the two troublemakers we've been tracking, though." I massage the conditioner through my hair, keeping half an eye on the open door through the steamed-up shower glass. I've caught David peeking before.

"How did you manage that? Bribery?" He sounds intrigued.

"Not really. They didn't violate anyone's privacy by actually naming names. But their description of 'that redhead diva bitch who claimed she got frostbite on her nose out of nowhere and then exploded when the surgeon said amputation might be necessary,' sounds a lot like Andrea Case. And 'that drunk biker who was in here twice in three days for frostbite and for getting maced by the other patient,' sounds an awful lot like Daniel Gates."

"That's a good point." More typing. "Oh, great...you finished the write-up of your interview with them last night?"

"Yeah, I wanted to get it down in writing while it was fresh." I hate interviews where they won't let me record.

"This is eight pages. No wonder you're worn out. What time did you finally get to sleep?" Now he sounds worried, which makes me feel a bit guilty.

I shake it off after a moment. "I wasn't looking at the clock."

"Tch. You work too hard." I hear one of the interviews start to play: the one with Jack.

"All right, so," I hear my own voice, which sounds tinny and strange in recordings. I try to ignore that as I listen. *"Please state your name, age, hometown, and occupation for the record."*

Jack's laughing voice takes over. *"My name's Jack Frost, as I told you before. I'm ageless, I live at the North Pole with my father Saint Nicholas, and my job is bringing the fall colors and the winter frosts."*

A long, awkward pause. *"I understand that you're in character for the kids and all, but—"*

"Oh, is that what I'm doing?" His tone teases me.

"Does this guy have to troll us each and every time that we get him on camera?" Delgado grumbles. "Hurry up. I want to go over this stuff with you before we grab some breakfast."

"I'm not entirely sure that he is trolling us," I say thoughtfully as I rinse out my hair. "He does have a weird sense of humor, but so does his dad, and these are the guys who made sure the local food bank had a surplus right before the holiday."

"Do you think he and his dad are delusional?" he asks seriously, stopping the video.

"I don't know. But if they are, it's the most benign delusion ever. As far as I can tell, pretty much everyone up here loves them, even if nobody past the age of five believes that they're anything but ordinary people." I finish the shower and close the door most of the way so that I can towel off and dress.

"Okay, yeah. I admit his dad is pretty cool. But I don't trust this guy." He hesitates then says slowly, "He's wasting our time. And he keeps hitting on you."

I stop short in the middle of pulling on my long underwear, hearing a faint alarm bell go off in the back of my head. He's not wrong; Jack is a flirt.

That's not the problem. The problem is that after all this

time, David should know better than to be jealous. And yet I'm hearing that tone in his voice.

It takes everything I have to keep the awkward laugh out of my own voice as I finish dressing. "He hits on every woman who's over the age of eighteen and isn't wearing a ring. What's your point?"

Another pause. "Oh." He sounds a little calmer suddenly, and I roll my eyes. "Well, he just annoys me."

"Yeah, well, he's a bit immature, and immaturity is annoying." So is jealousy, especially when it's coming from a guy who had his chance and blew it. "Give me a minute, and let's go over the new stuff before breakfast."

I have to get things back on track. If David is starting to think of me as his again—if he's getting jealous—then we have a problem. We're on the brink of proving the paranormal origin of an ongoing town-wide phenomenon. I don't have time for David's romantic regrets.

Or my own.

CHAPTER 2

David

"So according to the nurses, the biker was recovering from hypothermia and mild frostbite when he was picked up by state police." I lean toward the laptop screen with Andi beside me, trying to ignore how nice her freshly-washed hair smells. I really don't have time for inconvenient boners.

THE BIGGEST MISTAKE I have ever made in my life, contrary to the beliefs of my family, wasn't my getting into paranormal investigation when I'm not even a believer myself. And it also wasn't the time I blew a hundred thousand dollars of Dad's money in Monaco when I was twenty. It wasn't even when I let a former partner take one of my inventions as his severance—a patent that turned out to be worth millions.

IT WAS, quite simply, letting the woman of my dreams slip through my fingers.

Andromeda "Andi" Carter really is the whole package. Smart, ambitious, imaginative, hot, pretty, and sweet. At sixteen, I wanted to get into her pants so badly that I couldn't breathe, but of course, she put me off. At twenty, I finally did get into her pants—and I loved every minute of it. Not that there were ever too many minutes to savor at one time.

But Andi, well, she never seemed to enjoy it as much as I did. Which always frustrated me. At the time, I thought there was something wrong with her when she didn't like exactly what I liked in bed, when I liked it. But I was the typical selfish twenty-year-old guy back then with my brain mostly located at the end of my dick.

I know better now, but it's too late. Our problems in bed were just one of many other issues that drove us apart. Eight months after I made love to her for the first time, she packed her bags and left.

We patched things up enough to keep Astraea together as well as our friendship. But I still wonder to this day what would have happened if we'd waited until we both had grown up more. Would it have lasted? Would it last if we tried again now?

"How did you find out that Andrea Case was the one who maced him?" I ask Andi as I look up from her notes.

"They got into a fistfight in the waiting room." She winces as she speaks, and I stifle an outburst of laughter.

. . .

"Oh man, this town." I rub my face and look back at her notes. "Well, that does it for the written stuff. Let's have a look at the rest of yesterday's interviews and then grab some breakfast."

"Sounds good to me. I'm starving." She's sitting next to me brushing her hair out. The rich smell of her hair mixes with the fruity shampoo and tickles my nostrils. As much as I love the smell of her, I have to keep reminding myself that she's not mine.

Some days, I'm fine with that. Others, it's like a fucking Greek tragedy that I simply can't escape, leaving me wondering why I wasn't prescient enough to see the writing on the wall back then. Right now, being so close to Andi makes me want to slip an arm around her and beg her to take me back.

Ugh, too bad it's too early for a drink.

"So what's our amended timeline?" she asks as she pulls up a few interviews.

I bring the timeline file up on my smartphone. "December 23rd at dawn, the mistletoe appears. Nobody sees who put it up or who keeps replacing it when it's taken down. Mistletoe is everywhere including private houses and the interior of the church. The night of the 25th, a snowstorm hits, damaging outdoor decorations and blacking out half the town. When we dig out the next morning, the mistletoe had stayed up. Either it resisted wind that ripped branches off trees in a few places, or somehow someone put it all back up after the storm without being seen or leaving tracks in the snow."

It sounds absolutely ridiculous to me, except that I saw that last part with my own eyes. The stuff simply doesn't stay down for long. The pastor, who keeps clearing his grounds of mistletoe since he doesn't want people sucking face in the church graveyard, complained about it to me. He also mentioned, once again, that when it's replaced, no footprints are left in the snow.

That one detail—that one inexplicable thing—is what's kept me here even though this could be one of our most boring investigations yet. All we do most of the day is push through crowds and plod around chasing down rumors about what's happening. The mistletoe keeps reappearing over new snow with no footprints.

How bizarre is that?

"Is there any chance that the whole town is in on it? Maybe it's just a stunt to create this tourism boom?" I ask slowly and thoughtfully. "Or maybe as a little Christmas magic for the kids?"

She shakes her head after a brief, thoughtful silence. "No. It's created too much disruption. And because of how people react to it: everyone we interviewed seems baffled. If everyone was in on it, then a lot of the townspeople would have to be amazing amateur actors."

I SIT BACK, tapping my lips with my finger. The motive is plausible, but the execution...

SHE'S RIGHT. It would be impossible or nearly so. One of the Whitmans or someone else must have hired a small team of people who have been sneaking around. Or...something. I'm not crediting anything supernatural. Not yet.

"OKAY, we already have the transcripts of Jack's comments." She leans forward slightly as she brings his interview recording back up. It's stopped in the middle, frozen on a single frame of his irritatingly handsome face.

GOD, I hate this guy. Not just because he flirts with Andi in front of me, not just because he doesn't really seem to do anything useful with his time and wealth, but because Andi seems...interested. And I'm not handling that well.

EVEN THOUGH I'VE taken some casual lovers over the years, there's never been anyone else for me besides Andi. I think it might be the same for her—in fact, I don't think she's dated since she packed her bags and left our home. Maybe I should feel bad about that. I kind of worry that some of my behavior left her jaded about relationships.

. . .

Yeah. It was that big of a screw-up. I'm not proud of it.

There's part of me that gets stupid romantic sometimes and thinks that maybe Andi's never dated anyone else because she's been waiting for me to grow up. That maybe she'll give me another shot now that she knows I've got my shit together.

But that's probably stupid. I had my shot. I shouldn't be jealous if she decides to move on.

Except I really, really am jealous. I know it's a problem. I hope that she doesn't notice…but I know it's a slim hope. Andi notices everything.

Sitting side by side, we start playing through the interview with the sound on low, watching Jack Whitman's expressions and gestures. I never trust a guy that smiles that much, and I hope that Andi doesn't either. Fortunately, she's smart, and she doesn't put up with bad treatment.

She'll catch on to his bullshit soon enough and brush him off. Not that it's any of my business. After all, she's not mine anymore. *But I still give a shit about her, and this guy is bad news. I can feel it.*

"Hold on a second," she says, pausing the tape. "That shop window right there that he's leaning next to." She points to the window in question.

. . .

"That's the candy store. What am I looking at?"

"By his face." She taps the screen, and I peer at the image. Jack has leaned over against the storefront window and is blowing on it softly, the mist of his breath making a fern pattern of frost on the glass.

"Weird," she mumbles.

"What's weird? It's freezing, and he breathed on the glass. Of course it fogged up and then frosted over." I stare at the frost pattern, wondering just what it is that has captivated her. "I used to see them on the old shed at my grandmother's farmhouse every winter when I was a kid."

"It's not the frost itself. It's the form it's taking. Windows used to get that fern frond pattern on them in winter back in the days of single glazing, like on your grandmother's shed. But it shouldn't happen on a sheet of shop glass."

I'm not following. Maybe this is an upstate thing—she's the one who grew up around here. If anyone would know, it's her. "Why?"

"Almost all of the home and shop windows around here are double and triple glazed. They're a lot more insulated, so you don't get the level of heat loss that causes those patterns on the glass." She's toying with the end of her braid, looking thoughtful.

"Are you sure? Some of the buildings around here are really old—they could have the original glass." I try not to stare at her too obviously, but this is one of countless cute little gestures of hers that make me want to hug her—and drag her off to bed to show her what I've learned. I struggle to shift my focus back to the conversation.

She nods once. "Only one way to find out. I want to get a look at that shop window as soon as we have some food in us."

"Fair enough. Let's just...not do so much legwork outside today, all right? It's twelve degrees out."

She gives me a lopsided smile. "You were the one who was so eager to get going a half hour ago when you were dragging me out of bed. Now come on, we can warm up with cocoa breaks every now and again while we're out."

"As long as the cocoa is spiked." A man has to put his foot down sometime, and if I have to endure another day of pounding the streets of this tiny town in freezing weather, I'm not doing it totally sober.

"The warmth you get from booze is fake. You know that." She frowns at me worriedly, and I snort.

. . .

I shrug. "'Tis the fucking season." I shut down the laptop and get up to bundle into my outerwear.

Her frown dissolves and a twinkle of humor enters her eyes. "All right, fair enough."

CHAPTER 3

Andi

We're getting closer to the truth. I can feel it. The idea sings in my head as David and I load our plates at the breakfast buffet and take seats across from each other at a small table. "I'm pretty sure we're headed for a breakthrough," I say confidently as we settle in.

He looks up at me with dull sarcasm in his eyes that just screams, '*Are you kidding?*'

"Food, coffee," he mumbles around his first forkful of eggs. "No talk."

It stops me short, and I let out a little laugh as he scoops more of his scrambled eggs into his mouth. I take a bite of my waffles, and my own appetite wakes up.

. . .

We eat in silence for a while. It's easy and relaxed, not awkward like it was when I first broke up with him. On those mornings, sitting across from each other at my breakfast table in the Boston Tudor I've since sold, the silence between us was packed full of tension.

Now, we're just stuffing our faces with good country fare and a whole lot of coffee. Outside the window, snow is drifting down again. People crowd down the packed streets as if it were midsummer, bundled against the cold, trying to ignore the snow blowing into their faces.

Phoenicia sure is pretty. It's one of those little towns that you whip past on the highway, with its own sign and exit, but with hills and tall trees concealing large parts of the town. It's thriving compared to a lot of these isolated highway-side towns, mostly because it caters to tourists with businesses like the old-timey theater and river rafting.

But it's normally not thriving like this. The breakfast room is crowded. Parking spots are filled everywhere that I can see. And foot traffic is constantly being held up by the ever-present mistletoe with some couples stopping every couple of minutes to participate in the novelty.

It's pretty cute to watch—people stealing kisses in the cold. But it makes me a little sad, too. I see the way David looks at me when he thinks I don't notice, and it makes me wistful. I have always wondered what it would be like if I gave him a second chance. It just never seemed...smart. So I never tried it.

But times like this, watching the little scenes of romance and the awkwardness of young love on the snowy street, I'm reminded too much of my cold and lonely bed. Sometimes I miss him, though I tell myself I just miss having someone at my side who cares about me. No matter how frustrated David made me, at least I always knew that he gave a damn. And I know that he always will—even if he sometimes has no idea at all how to express it.

"You know," he says finally, once he's caffeinated enough that his eyes aren't dull, "there's one thing I haven't asked you. What exactly is the theory we're working from in this case?"

"Sorry, what?" I ask distractedly. I just noticed Jack outside. He's idly gliding along in his boots down a strip of ice that has formed after repeated passes by the plows. His hands are tucked behind his back, his midnight blue coat and dark hair flap in the breeze, and he's smiling with mischievous amusement.

Of course he grabs my attention easily. Jack has...glamour. That's the only way I can describe it. I have been in the presence of millionaires, scientific geniuses, industry giants, and movie stars...but Jack manages to outshine them all—without seeming to make much of an effort.

. . .

Who is he really? I wonder, and then catch myself and look back at David.

"Are we here because there's simply another kind of unknown phenomenon going on? If that's the case, what are we saying that phenomenon is? We have to go beyond a 'Christmas miracle' and get at some specifics." He stabs at one of his sausages as I tear my eyes away from the gorgeous man gliding past...yet again.

His question catches me by surprise. I'm not sure I've ever given him a working theory beyond telling him, *"This is obviously supernatural. Let's see what we can catch on tape."* On the other hand, we've never spent over a week in the cold, away from our families on the holidays, to chase what could be our first real proof of the supernatural. Nor has it ever been this big, with this many witnesses.

"Give me a moment," I mutter over the rim of my coffee mug. "This is a little hard to put into words."

"It always is," he grumbles, and I feel a stab of worry. He sees my face and just offers a tight smile. "Sorry. I'm just sick of the snow. Can't we just go ghost hunting in New Orleans for a few months?"

"That's actually damn tempting," I admit as the tension breaks, and he lets out a little laugh. "No, seriously. You're right.

We're probably going to end up presenting on this at the conventions, so I had better have my thoughts organized."

HE NODS SLOWLY and waits for me, staring broodingly out the window. I catch the exact moment that he notices Jack: his expression darkens, his eyes narrow slightly. I swallow and look down at the tabletop, trying to gather my thoughts.

In all the years we've been doing this—meticulously cataloging supernatural events and testing their validity, publishing books, giving talks at conventions, and interviews for blogs and podcasts—there's never been one single big discovery like this. No 'Aha!' moment where we absolutely knew we had proof that people would have to believe. Plenty of hopeful moments—and a lot of letdowns—but we've never found our Holy Grail.

WE'VE COME CLOSE: the haunted house in North Carolina with the constant scrambling sounds in its walls but no signs of infestation; the San Francisco vampire that really did have what looked to be a photo of himself from 1863—even if David swears to this day that the guy in the picture was just a doppelganger.

WE'VE COME BACK from our investigations with proof that impresses those in our field, and we've managed to make a name for ourselves among American parapsychologists. The problem is that we can never convince *everyone* to let go of their preconceived beliefs and take in new information. No matter how convincing our evidence, people always want to run it through their cultural, religious, and personal filters—just like David does.

And that's what makes our job so challenging. It's also

helped us learn how to cover all our tracks and be meticulous about our research and theories.

"The only working theory that I have so far is that whoever is responsible for this, their motives would be the same regardless of whether or not they are using some kind of supernatural ability to pull this off. It's a boost to the town—its economy, its reputation, its celebration of the holiday…" I'm rambling, I realize. I go quiet, cheeks heating up a little.

He sits forward. "Okay, that part I can get behind. Go on."

"Our prime suspects are Jack and his father, Dr. Whitman. Do we even know if their familial connection has ever been confirmed?" A lot of the local 'information' on people seems to be based on assumptions and rumors.

I'm used to the New York rumor mill; it churns 24/7 in small towns and big cities. It is even worse on the Internet: from whispers in boardrooms to breathless social media posts by tween girls, it runs an endless stream of what-ifs, fluff, filler, and bullshit—and sometimes, the occasional gem. Like the collection of local folklore surrounding the Whitmans.

"Very little about Dr. Whitman is confirmed, except for his history of propping up the town every winter with donations, benefits, and parties. As for Jack, he has a confirmed career as a hotshot local skier and playboy with a whole lot of awards and prizes." He's reading from the file on his phone.

THAT MAKES me feel better about spending so much time getting everything updated last night. I wasn't sleeping anyway, but it is still nice to know that I spent my bout of insomnia being productive. "Nobody's entirely sure what kind of doctor Whitman is, though. Some say he has a PhD in folklore, some says he's a pediatrician, some say he's a child psychologist. There's a whole list. Scroll down two pages," I tell him.

"OH WAIT." He flicks his finger over his phone screen and pauses to swallow down more coffee.

I'M STILL WORKING on my eggs. I've been eating more slowly than usual, my attention all over the place, what with the investigation, the holiday, David, Jack, the sex dreams I've been having about both of them since we got here...

I COVER my face with my hands, blushing furiously. I've been trying not to think about those, especially in David's presence.

IT'S TRUE, though. It's the reason I couldn't sleep last night. Better that I lose sleep than wake up feeling that way again—heated but unsatisfied, but mostly frustrated as hell from the images my mind teases me with.

. . .

But I can't help it. My head keeps filling up with images and sensations that have never happened, but that I wish would. If only things were different.

In one dream, I'm wrestling with Jack on an honest to God pile of furs over who gets to be on top. He's laughing playfully and letting me win...sometimes. There's snow falling outside the odd little cottage, and the icy draft whistling past the window panes bites any bit of my skin not covered by the furs—or him—but the heat inside of me seems to burn it away.

And then there are the dreams about David. David making me feel pleasure for hours on end, instead of turning me on and then leaving me lying there cold, confused, and frustrated.

Though my dream self doesn't seem to have any issues finding release, my real self isn't so lucky. I don't know how it feels to climax, and no matter how hot my dreams are, my body just won't go that far on images alone. I keep waking up shaking and sweaty—aching with unfulfilled need.

I don't like dwelling on David's failings as a husband, because if I do I end up getting this stabbing headache in my temples that I can't get rid of for hours. And then I can't handle being around David for a while.

I remind myself of a few things as I wait for David to finish skimming the file. It helps keep my old frustrations at bay.

. . .

First, after our breakup and after spending a few years speaking to other women about their own failed romances, I learned that David was pretty typical of early twenties guys—both in bed and out. I could have forgiven his flakiness, his goofiness, and even the sexual inexperience if he had been willing to admit to it, to listen, and to learn. But he was convinced he knew everything already, and I quickly got too frustrated to deal with that.

Turns out, most young guys seem to think they know everything about sex—or are at least too proud to admit that they don't.

If only I had known, I might have been more patient and kept trying. Or I would have at least found another way to approach the subject.

In my dreams, I get a taste of what might have happened if I had. And it's heartbreaking.

I've never had an orgasm in my life. For a while after our relationship ended, David's voice stayed in my head, blaming me for being 'uptight.' It lingered, even though I had fought back at the time, demanding to know what a guy with an 'I'm going in dry' T-shirt could possibly know about satisfying women.

. . .

IN THE END, we both lost. I learned the hard way not to get too serious too fast, especially when you're just starting out. Knowing someone as a friend and knowing them as a lover and potential husband, it turns out, are two very, very different things.

DAVID LEARNED the hard way that if you can't please your woman, and you don't want to learn, then you don't get to blame her for that. You don't call her frigid, you don't ask what's wrong with her, and you don't otherwise add insult to injury by being a shitty lover and then calling her one.

And if you do, then you'd better get ready for her to unload six months of sexual frustration, humiliation, and heartbreak at you in one five-minute verbal barrage, and then watch her turn around and start packing her things.

I SHAKE myself out of my reverie to see that David is chuckling obliviously, probably over some of the Whitman folklore I gathered while he was interviewing some of the store owners. I surreptitiously wipe my eyes, face turned toward the window. Jack is out there, chatting and laughing a little with a big biker guy that I peg after a second as Daniel Gates's brother, Aaron.

AARON SEEMS to be in an awfully good mood for a guy whose brother went straight from the hospital to jail recently. Curiosity distracts me enough that some of my sadness lifts. My failure to launch with David is in the past, after all. I've already decided not to let it ruin the present.

. . .

How I wish I could have had just one single night with him that was even half as good as my dreams.

If you want to continue reading this story, you can get your copy from your favorite vendor by searching for the title:

A Kiss of Winter

A Second Chance Christmas Romance
(Dreams Fulfilled Book 3)

You can also find the e-book version by typing this link in your computer's browser:

https://www.hotandsteamyromance.com/products/a-kiss-of-winter-a-second-chance-christmas-romance

OTHER BOOKS BY THIS AUTHOR

Saving Her Rescuer: A Billionaire & A Virgin Romance

I was just trying to get away from my crazy ex for the weekend when I ended up in a giant pileup on the highway up to Gore Mountain.

https://geni.us/SavingHerRescuer

∽

Sensual Sounds: A Rockstar Ménage

Lust. Lies. Double lives.

The rock and roll industry is full of people who are looking out for themselves and willing to do anything to rise to the top.

https://www.hotandsteamyromance.com/collections/frontpage/products/sensual-sounds-a-rockstar-menage

∽

On the Run: A Secret Baby Romance

Murder. Lies. Fraud. Just another day in the lives of billionaires and women on the run.

https://www.hotandsteamyromance.com/collections/frontpage/products/on-the-run-a-secret-baby-romance

∽

The Dirty Doctor's Touch: A Billionaire Doctor Romance

I am a master. An elitist. I am at the top of my field, and I know what I am doing.

https://www.hotandsteamyromance.com/collections/frontpage/products/the-dirty-doctor-s-touch-a-billionaire-doctor-romance

∽

The Hero She Needs: A Single Daddy Next Door Romance

He's the only man I've ever wanted...

https://www.hotandsteamyromance.com/collections/frontpage/products/the-hero-she-needs-a-single-daddy-next-door-romance

∽

You can find all of my books here

Hot and Steamy Romance
https://www.hotandsteamyromance.com

∽

Facebook

facebook.com/HotAndSteamyRomance

COPYRIGHT

©Copyright 2020 by Scarlett King- All rights Reserved

In no way is it legal to reproduce, duplicate, or transmit any part of this document in either electronic means or in printed format. Recording of this publication is strictly prohibited and any storage of this document is not allowed unless with written permission from the publisher. All rights are reserved.

Respective authors own all copyrights not held by the publisher.

www.ingramcontent.com/pod-product-compliance
Lightning Source LLC
LaVergne TN
LVHW011721060526
838200LV00051B/2984